Ma
Supe

Marshall Mulgrew's Supernatural Mysteries
© 2017 Mark A. Roeder

Cover Photo Credit: Pexels.com

Cover Design: Ken Clark

ISBN-13: 978-1546876588

ISBN-10: 1546876588

Acknowledgments

No one writes a novel alone. I've been lucky enough to have several proofreaders correct my many mistakes over the years. Those who have been at it the longest and most consistently are Ken Clark and James Adkinson. I'm not sure what I would do without them. Ken also designs all my covers and does a wonderful job. David Tedesco has joined these two more recently and together the three tremendously improve my novels. I cannot even begin to express how thankful I am for the long hours of work they dedicate to my books.

Also look for audiobook versions on Amazon.com and Audible.com

Blackford Gay Youth Chronicles:

Outfield Menace

Snow Angel

The Nudo Twins

Phantom World

Second Star to the Right

The Perfect Boy

Verona Gay Youth Chronicles:

Ugly

Beautiful

The Soccer Field Is Empty

Someone Is Watching

A Better Place

The Summer of My Discontent

Disastrous Dates & Dream Boys

Just Making Out

Temptation University*

Scarecrows

The Fat Kid

Brendan & Casper: Older & Better

Light in the Darkness

Bloomington Gay Youth Chronicles

A Triumph of Will

Temptation University*

The Picture of Dorian Gay

Yesterday's Tomorrow

Boy Trouble

The New Bad Ass in Town

Bloomington Boys—Brandon & Dorian*

Bloomington Boys—Nathan & Devon*

Bloomington Boys—Scotty & Casper*

Bloomington Boys—Tim & Marc*

Peralta's Bike Shop

Hate at First Sight

A Boy Toy for Christmas

*Crossover novels that fit into two series

Other Novels:

Cadets of Culver

Fierce Competition

The Vampire's Heart

Homo for the Holidays

For more information on current and upcoming novels go to markroeder.com.

Mad as a Hatter

Chapter One
Verona, Indiana
October 2007

Cold rain hit the glass as I gazed out the window of my room on the third floor in the Graymoor Mansion. A small fire crackled in the hearth, despite the fact it was early October. I could see little out the window except the shadows of the oak limbs below as they swayed in the breeze. It was the perfect night for ghostly activity... or a murder.

A loud knock at the door disturbed my musings. I walked across the rugs on the hardwood floor and opened it.

"Marshall, there are two guys downstairs who want to talk to you. They're from the FBI," Sean said.

I arched my brows. I was accustomed to dealing with ghosts and the supernatural, but the FBI?

I shrugged and stepped out into the hall with Sean. "What have you done this time Marshall? Have you been digging up graves again?" Sean grinned. We had known each other since high school. His family owned the mansion and Sean ran it as a bed & breakfast.

"No. Well, not recently."

Sean eyed me, trying to figure out if I was kidding or not. I liked to keep him guessing.

We climbed down two flights of stairs into the enormous parlor that acted as a lobby for the bed & breakfast. It was filled with Victorian sofas, chairs, and marble-topped tables. A fire crackled in the fireplace to ward off the chill.

"I put them in the study so you'll have privacy."

"Thanks Sean."

I crossed the parlor and opened the door to the study, a walnut-paneled room with heavy hunter green drapes and bookshelves covering most of the wall space. Two men wearing suits stood when I entered.

"Marshall Mulgrew?"

I nodded.

"I'm Agent Heck. This is Agent Freeman."

They showed me their ID's but they could have been fakes for all I knew. I'd never met an FBI agent before. That was the stuff of films and TV.

"What can I do for you?" I asked.

"Do you remember a Carla Mason?"

I thought for a moment and then smiled.

"Yes, she hired me about eight months ago. Is she okay?"

"She's fine."

"Good. I enjoyed working with her family. Her boys are hilarious. They were frightened at the time, but intensely curious about what was going on."

"I know. They're my nephews. Carla is my sister. She recommended you."

"So... why are you here?"

I gestured to the Victorian armchairs and we all sat down.

"We would like to hire you as a special investigator. There have been a series of murders that frankly, we can't explain."

"Murders? You know I'm not a detective. Right? I work with the supernatural, not murder. I didn't know the FBI got involved in such cases."

"We don't. That's precisely why we need you."

"Tell me more."

"During the last several months there have been a series of murders that defy rational explanation. They have occurred in various locations in the Midwest and are disturbingly similar. In the most recent case the victim was found strangled to death in her apartment on the eighth floor. There was no evidence of forced entry. In fact, all windows were locked and the door was locked with a chain from the inside. While the victim could have let the murderer in, we have no idea how he or she could have exited again. The police had to break the chain to get in."

"And it wasn't a suicide?"

"The victim was strangled, but no murder weapon was found. If she killed herself whatever she used would still have been in the apartment, unless someone removed it."

"Which they could not have done."

"You see our problem."

"I'm interested," I said.

"So you think there may be a supernatural explanation?"

I was surprised indeed to hear this question from the lips of an FBI agent.

"I think it's likely, unless you've missed something. I'm not a detective, but I don't see how a human could have committed the murder."

Agent Freeman looked skeptical, but Agent Heck nodded.

"I take it you are familiar with the events at your sister's house," I said.

"That's why we came to you. To be honest, I thought all this supernatural stuff was a load of bullshit, but... my sister doesn't lie and she's a rational individual. She was a skeptic as well until something unseen shoved her down the stairs."

"That's usually the way it goes. Nearly everyone is a skeptic until they witness or experience a supernatural event themselves."

"I'm afraid I don't share Agent Heck's confidence in this matter. There are no such things as ghosts."

"It's probably not wise to say that in this house." Before I could even begin to explain Agent Freeman bolted from his chair and a boyish giggle filled the air.

"What the hell was that?" Agent Freeman said, clearly frightened.

"One of the ghosts you don't believe exists. Etienne, behave yourself."

"Yes, Marshall."

Agent Freeman's chair slid toward him. He jumped back, but then approached and carefully checked it out, no doubt looking for wires or a mechanism that could explain the movement. He did not sit down again. Both agents were a bit pale.

"How did you do that?"

"I didn't. Etienne did."

"There is no such thing as a... oww! Something pinched my butt!"

Agent Heck laughed as his partner rubbed his ass.

"You'd better not say that again. Etienne doesn't always do what I say."

Etienne giggled and Agent Freeman twisted around trying to figure out where he was.

"Sit down. We're wasting time," said Agent Heck.

His partner did so cautiously and spent the remainder of his time looking around the study uneasily. Luckily, Etienne behaved himself.

"I believe and I've convinced the department to take you on," said Agent Heck. "We would like you to become a special agent for this case, sort of a deputy if you will for investigative purposes only. We can provide you with credentials and ID that will allow you access to crime scenes and records connected to the cases in question. We'll compensate you, of course."

"Let's discuss details," I said.

For the next hour we did just that. The agents also presented me with two thick folders that contained copies of all pertinent documents and crime scene photos for the two most recent murders, both of which had occurred in the same town only days apart.

Sean and Skye were lingering in the lobby when we came out of the study. Agent Freeman glanced uneasily about the room, much to Agent Heck's amusement, but Heck wasn't quite at ease himself. I showed them to the door where we shook hands.

"We will be in touch in a couple of days and bring you everything you'll need," Agent Heck said.

I nodded and they departed.

"Well, they didn't take him out in handcuffs so I guess he's not running a drug ring," Skye said.

"My money was on prostitution. I figured he was running a whore house somewhere," Sean said.

"Funny guys."

"So what did they want?" Sean asked.

"Me. You are looking at the newest FBI agent."

The look on Sean and Skye's face was priceless.

"You can't be serious," Sean said.

"I am, but I won't exactly be an FBI agent. I'll be a special agent investigating a series of murders that are likely related to the supernatural. I'm not allowed to arrest or shoot anyone."

"Where's the fun in that?" Sean asked, grinning.

"I knew weirdness would involve itself somehow," Skye said. "Of course, the FBI coming to you is weird in itself."

"I have to agree with you there, but this is a case in my field. There have been a series of murders committed in locked rooms."

"What's supernatural about that?" Skye asked.

"The rooms were locked from the inside. The FBI has been unable to determine how a murderer could get back out after committing the crime."

"Suicides?" Sean asked.

"While that is the obvious answer, suicide has been ruled out. The victims were murdered, but in each case the murderer could not have left the crime scene and no murderer was found, so either the FBI has missed something or the cause is supernatural."

"That does sound fascinating," Skye said.

"Good, because when I start investigating, I'd like you to come with me."

"Me? Oh, I get it, you'd miss me too much."

"Um, no, but it could be dangerous to go into this alone."

"And you need some muscle," Skye said, flexing his arm. His bicep bulged.

"Possibly, but mostly I need someone to watch my back and we've worked well together in the past."

"Do I get a badge?"

"We'll see."

Sean laughed because Skye was clearly excited.

"I'm going to my room to review this material. The agents said they'd be back in a couple of days. I'll give Agent Heck a call and see if I can get you some ID Skye."

"Then you can play dress up," Sean said, patting him on the back. Skye shot him a fake glare.

My head was spinning as I walked up the stairs, not because of the FBI involvement, but because of the case itself. I had investigated many hauntings and disturbances over the years. Often the cause was quite natural, but at other times I turned up something truly supernatural. I could feel in my gut that this was one of those times.

I spent most of the next two days going over the files the agents left with me. They were extensive and detailed. The crime scene photos of the corpses would have disturbed most, but I frequently saw worse. I possessed some psychic abilities and among these was the ability to see the dead. If that freaks you out you might as well stop reading because I'm not kidding. I see dead people, just like Haley Joel Osment in *The Sixth Sense*. Often, I see the dead as they looked at the moment of their death and the sight was sometimes gruesome.

I started with the assumption that the killer was human. I believed the murderer was not, but my first goal was to eliminate all natural possibilities. That's where I usually start because there are often natural explanations for seemingly supernatural events.

I went through all the material and tried to think of any way a living being could have committed the murder and exited the locked rooms. The thoroughness of the FBI helped greatly. When I came up with the possibility the murderer had exited through an air vent, I was quickly able to conclude from the measurements taken that the air vents were too small and from the photos that the grills were firmly in place.

The cause had to be supernatural. The most likely candidate was a spirit. While most had extreme difficulty becoming visible, let alone being able to manipulate physical objects, there were those who could achieve an actual physical form for a short time. The ability was rare and unfortunately it was the most violent spirits who usually achieved it.

Another possibility was a changeling. I had never encountered one, and there was debate in scholarly circles about whether or not they actually existed, or had existed, or were pure myth. Virtually all myths are based in fact, but the facts are often vastly different from reality. Few realize that Dracula, King Arthur, and Robin Hood were actual historical individuals. The truth of their existence was far removed from the myths, but each was quite real. The changeling myths are no doubt based in fact, but how far the legends had drifted from fact I did not know.

There are certain elemental spirits that might be capable of pulling off a murder, but it was not likely. There were other supernatural suspects, but I intended to start with the most likely. If I ruled out ghosts, I would delve more deeply into other supernatural possibilities.

***

"Seriously? You want us to ride in *that*?" Skye asked when he spotted my hearse parked in front of Graymoor Mansion.

"Why are you complaining? You love vintage cars."

"Not cars that carry dead people."

"Hey, the original owners of your '35 Auburn are dead."

"Yes, but they didn't ride in it after they died. Besides, I don't think Colin will want to be seen in this car."

"We're taking the hearse? Sweet!" Colin said when he came out the front doors of the mansion. I grinned at Skye.

"Shut up."

"You'll love my baby Skye. It is a Cadillac and it's a 1964 model so you can't say it's not vintage. It's also very comfy."

"Is there room for all of us in the front seat?"

"There is plenty of room, but if you want to stretch out you can ride in the back."

"No thank you."

Colin tossed his bags into the back and Skye reluctantly followed suit. Colin climbed in the passenger side and Skye slid in beside him.

"See? Plenty of room."

"This will be a blast!" Colin said.

Skye didn't comment as I started up the hearse and pulled around the drive. Colin was definitely enthused. Colin was Skye's nephew. He was only sixteen, but had lived in Graymoor Mansion over a year since the death of his mother and step-father so he was well acquainted with the supernatural. He even had a pet ghost-cat. Those of us who live in Graymoor are an odd lot and I'm not telling you even half of it. Colin was on fall break from high school, so Skye decided to bring him along. I would have balked if it was any other boy, but Colin could handle himself in tight situations. I was basically now traveling with two bodyguards.

"Are we there yet?" Colin asked as we pulled out of town.

"I will stop this car right here. I swear!" I said, trying my best to sound like a frustrated dad. Colin laughed.

17

"Where are we headed?" he asked.

"We're staying at the Biddle Hotel."

"What? A hotel? You couldn't find a nice funeral home where we could stay?" Skye asked.

"That could be fun, but no. You'll like the hotel. It's on campus."

"Indiana University?" Colin asked.

"Yeah."

"Cool. College boys and girls. Mmm."

"You're too young for anyone who goes to IU and you're sharing a room with me, so forget it," Skye said.

"Ha! You want a college boy yourself! I'll make a deal with you. I'll get lost when you want the room for a hookup if you'll do the same for me."

"No deal. Besides, we're going to work."

"There is always time for fun."

"What is it with you gay and bi guys?" I asked.

"He sounds frustrated. I pity heteros," Skye said.

"Don't you though?"

"Shut up. There will be no ganging up on me."

I loved driving my hearse. It was a luxurious automobile and had plenty of room in the back for all my equipment and research materials. I loved the styling of the car, from the short fins at the rear to the sleek black exterior, to the original white curtains and interior of the back. I knew a hearse didn't suit everyone's taste, but it was the perfect car for me.

The drive was pleasant and I had no trouble finding The Biddle Hotel, which was located inside the student union. A great many Verona boys had attended IU, but Skye had graduated from USC and I went to school in Great Britain. The British accent I had picked up during my school years sometimes returned without warning.

We parked in the lot next to the building and drew a few stares as we climbed out of the hearse. The hotel lobby was on the near end, which was a good thing because the building was massive. It housed not only the hotel, but meeting rooms, lounges, at least one theatre, restaurants, shops, and offices. It is the largest student union in the world.

We checked in and took an elevator to our fifth floor adjoining rooms. I wasn't checking out the crime scene until the next day so we had some free time. Brendan and some of the other IU alumni had clued us in to the major sites and best restaurants. Brendan graduated way back in 1986, but Brendan and Casper visited Bloomington from time to time and some of the restaurants were still in business.

"Are you guys hungry yet?" I said as we walked down the hallway to our rooms.

"I'm always hungry," Colin said.

"I could eat, but I want to look around campus a little first," Skye said.

"He wants to check out college boys," Colin said.

"No, but I'm sure you do."

"We both do," Colin said then grinned.

"Let's dump our bags and then meet back in the hall," I said.

We entered our adjoining rooms. Mine was small, but very comfortable and pleasant. I had a view of campus to the east. I could mostly see trees, but spotted a few buildings in the distance. When I looked almost straight down I spotted a small graveyard. Curious.

The guys were already waiting when I stepped into the hallway. Instead of taking the elevator we took the stairs and promptly got lost.

"Casper was right. This building is confusing. I should have listened more closely when he was talking about it," Skye said.

Since we were exploring, it didn't much matter that we were lost. I generally spotted something of interest no matter my location. There were wonderful paintings displayed on walls, including several by the Indiana artist T.C. Steele, but my attention was drawn more to the supernatural.

The student union was filled with students walking the halls, studying, talking, and laughing, but the dead were also active here. My eyes locked for a few moments with those of a college boy who appeared to be from the 1950's. He smiled at me knowingly. I often helped spirits who were lost find their way, but this boy was not lost. He knew he was dead and was here because this is where he wished to be. He would move on when it suited him. Skye, Colin, and the students around us did not see him. There was an entire world that most missed. I pitied them and yet my ability to see the dead could be a burden at times.

"This is that place Brendan said we have to try," Skye said, pausing.

The Tudor Room was closed, but we peered through the windows of the doors. I could see tables covered with linen cloths, tapestries and paintings on the walls, and a grand piano.

"They'll be open for lunch tomorrow. We'll go then," I said.

We continued on and soon entered a large lounge filled with sofas and chairs. Nearly every seat was occupied. I smiled as we passed a boy lying on a sofa, snoring. There was a limestone fireplace with a fire merrily blazing away. A few students were gathered around it and so were the dead. An old man stood gazing at the flames and a college boy who looked like he was probably from the 1980's sat before the hearth. Both seemed content. I could always sense when a spirit needed my help. Many came straight toward me seeking assistance if they were lost. I knew that these ghosts did not need me.

We continued on out of the lounge. We passed a Starbuck's with a long line of student's waiting on our right.

"I think there is a Starbuck's everywhere. I keep expecting one to open in my bathroom," Skye said.

"And he hates coffee," Colin said.

"Hey, I like the scent. I just don't want to drink it."

We exited the building to the south and entered the old part of campus. I spotted even more spirits here. Indiana University was well over a century old and had plenty of time to gather ghosts. Students, professors, and others from years past walked along the sidewalks, sat on benches, and even conversed with each other. I frequently saw the dead, but it was unusual to see so many who were content. The dead were often restless, lost, angry, or confused, but I sensed none of that here. The spirits present must have truly loved this place.

"Uh, Marshall?" Colin asked.

I looked toward him. Colin and Skye were several feet ahead.

"He was lost in the other world again," Skye said.

"It's not another world. It's the same world. You just can't see it."

"There are ghosts here?" Colin asked, completely unafraid. Colin was quite accustomed to ghosts, although he could not see them as I did, except for his cat, which continued to perplex me.

"Many."

I caught up and we walked on. A beautiful grove in all its autumn glory stood before us and on its edge a small limestone pavilion. I held my hand out toward it.

"What?" Skye asked.

"This structure... it's a portal."

"To where?" Skye asked.

"I don't know, but it's a gateway."

That was as much as I could say because that was as much as I could sense.

"Is it dangerous?" Skye asked. He was no doubt thinking of the room of doorways hidden deep inside Graymoor Mansion.

"I don't believe so, but there is magic here."

"Cool," Colin said.

I stepped into the structure. A bronze plaque indicated it was the Rose Well House and talked about the donor, Theodore Rose. There was something familiar about the name, but I couldn't place it. It had nothing to do with my current mission in any case.

Skye entered more cautiously for he had experience with such things. Colin did not hesitate to step inside.

"Oh. Brendan said this was his favorite spot on campus. He used to study here," I said, remembering.

"I like it," Colin said.

I watched as the ghost of an older, portly man walked down the brick pathway and entered the pavilion. He paused only long enough to smile and nod at me and then walked on. I recognized him from the bronze statue that even now I could see in the near distance.

I didn't mention the ghost, but led Skye and Colin to the little circular stone plaza bordered by beds of roses. Benches sat in front of the raised beds and sitting on one of them was the bronze statue of the ghost I had just seen. I read the name on the plaque—Herman Wells. Brendan had mentioned meeting the living Herman Wells and how he never failed to remember

Brendan when their paths crossed on rare occasions after his college years. He was the president of IU at one time.

We soon moved on, gazing at the huge old buildings—Owen, Wiley and Kirkwood Halls and more.

"I wish we had more time. There is a lot of history here and a lot of activity."

"One case at time Marshall," Skye said. I grinned.

"My stomach says it's time to eat!" Colin noted.

"Okay. Okay. Let's head for the car."

"Car. Ha!" Skye said.

Several college girls and a few boys checked out Skye and Colin as we walked through campus. Both tended to turn heads wherever they went. Skye was probably the best looking guy I had ever seen and Colin was a younger version of him. Both were model good-looking and incredibly well built. I wasn't attracted to guys, but even I was aware of their beauty. I laughed when one college boy ran into another while checking out uncle and nephew.

"What?" Colin asked, who had missed it.

"You and Skye have an admirer and he rear ended another boy checking you out."

Colin look back, but the boy was gone.

"Rear ended Marshall?" Skye asked.

"You know what I mean!"

"Hey, look. Marshall's home away from home," Colin said as we came around the side of the student union and the graveyard I had spotted from my room came into view. There was also a small stone chapel.

"Eh, there's nothing to see here," I said.

"No ghosts?" Colin said.

"They seldom hang around cemeteries. They generally stick to the place they died, or around a loved one, or some location that was special to them, which seems to be the case with the ghosts I've seen here so far."

"How many have you seen?" Colin asked.

"I lost count at fifty."

"I wish I could see the dead."

"Be careful what you wish for. It's not always pleasant. Sometimes, it's gruesome," I warned.

"Yeah, and one freak in our group is enough," Skye said, then grinned mischievously.

I scratched the side of my head with my middle finger. Skye laughed.

"So, where are we eating?" Colin asked.

"How about the China Buffet? You can pig out. Brendan and Casper recommended it," I said.

"I'm in," Colin said.

"Yeah, that's one of our must eat-at restaurants. Isn't it?" Skye asked.

"Yes, it and the Tudor Room were at the top."

We were soon at the parking lot. I unlocked the hearse and then closed my eyes and stood still for a moment. I sensed something here, not ghosts, but memories from long ago. In my mind I saw baseball players in old-fashioned uniforms playing ball. That was unusual for me. I was capable of limited mind reading, but I seldom picked up on past events. A great deal of energy must have been expended in this place. Luckily, it was positive energy. I said nothing about it when I climbed in the car.

"Do you know where the China Buffet is?" Skye asked.

"Trust me."

"Yeah, I've heard *that* before."

Colin laughed.

I drove out of the parking lot and down 7th Street. I vaguely remembered Brendan's directions. Soon, we were on 10th Street, heading east. I turned south on Union Street. From there I made a few more turns.

"I think he's lost. We will starve before we get there," Skye said.

"And you are wrong again. That is 3rd Street," I said pointing to the cross street at the stoplight.

I turned and then soon turned again into Eastland Plaza. There was the China Buffet in the middle of a strip mall.

"Okay, so we might make it before we starve," Skye said.

We parked and walked inside. If the scent in the air was any indication, the food was going to be outstanding.

We paid, claimed a booth, and hit the buffet. I tried some honey chicken, seafood delight, sweet & sour chicken, salmon, and a few other items from the buffet. Soon, we were all seated. Skye and Colin both had heaped plates.

"Why aren't you both fat?" I asked.

"Because we work out and muscle burns calories," Skye said. "You could eat more if you worked out regularly."

"I'll pass. I don't need an enlarged ego."

"I think he's insulting us," Skye said to Colin. "It's hard to be humble when you're as hot as us."

Skye and Colin exchanged a high five. I laughed. I knew their conceit was an act for my entertainment.

"This is great. It's no wonder Brendan and Casper ate here a lot," I said.

"Yeah and it's cheap, an important point for college boys," Skye said.

"I almost feel like an outsider since most of the Verona guys, especially the older ones went to IU," I said.

"Not me. I would not trade my years at USC for anything," Skye said

"I might go to IU. I like their wrestling program," Colin said.

"I don't know, Colin. California is filled with blonds."

"Well, I like what I've seen here so far." Colin grinned. He was much like his uncle.

Our conversation waned as we concentrated more on our food. Skye and Colin each made another trip to the buffet and then yet another for ice cream. My first plate of food was plenty for me, but I did get hot tea and ice cream with chocolate syrup. We were all well stuffed by the time we departed.

There was a mall across the street, but we decided to save it for another day. We returned to the hotel, where we parted. Skye and Colin planned to explore more, but I wanted to review the file on the Bloomington cases to make sure I wasn't missing anything.

I made myself some hot tea and set to work, but I had gone over everything so thoroughly this was only a review. Even so, as

I reexamined the facts I was even more certain than ever that the supernatural was at work.

Among the effects of the victim was a receipt found on her desk for a Victorian calling card case. There was a photocopy of the receipt in the file. Something seemed familiar about the address of the antique shop where she had purchased it only days before her death. Perhaps... I checked the list the FBI had given me of murders that had occurred under similar circumstances and there it was. The antique shop was second on my list of crime scenes to check in Bloomington. Was there a connection or was it coincidence?

After reviewing the file, I watched TV for a while and then turned in early. I wanted to be sharp for the next day.

I awakened in the morning with plenty of time to shower and get ready. We were all on our own for breakfast, so I headed down to the mezzanine level and purchased myself a blueberry muffin and hot chocolate for breakfast from Sugar & Spice, another of Brendan and Casper's recommendations. The muffin was huge.

I took my food to a large eating area down the hall called The Common's. There were dozens of tables and most were empty. I guess the college crowd didn't like to get up early. I hadn't been fond of morning in my college years, although the school I attended was non-traditional. While my friends went off to universities, I went to the Blackwood School in Lincolnshire, England. It was a school for those with psychic abilities.

My blueberry muffin was excellent, especially with the hot chocolate. I observed the few college students present as I ate. They looked so young; more like high school kids. Did I ever look that young? I was only twenty-four, but some of the boys sitting near looked like kids.

I knocked on Skye's door an hour later. He answered wearing a towel.

"You never miss a chance to show off your body, do you Skye?" I teased.

"I thought you deserved a treat."

"Please. I just ate."

"Come in. I'll be ready in a minute. Colin is primping in the bathroom."

"I heard that!" came a muffled yell.

Skye dropped his towel. Damn, I wished my body looked that good, but then again I didn't think I wanted to put in the effort. I was far too lazy for defined abs.

Skye was fully dressed in under a minute.

"How do you do that?" I asked.

"Practice. It was especially useful in my college years."

"I'm not asking why."

"Good. You don't want to know the answer."

Colin came out of the bathroom. He was fully dressed with not a hair out of place. Were all gay guys so fastidious or only the gorgeous ones? Then again, Colin was bi, not gay.

"You want to come with us Colin or do you have something better to do?" I asked.

"I'm going to hang out on campus."

"Stay out of trouble," Skye said.

"Me?"

"Yes. You. Remember, I used to be you. I already know what you're thinking. Don't even think about it."

Colin rolled his eyes.

"Meet us at the Tudor Room at noon or we're eating without you," I said.

"I'll be there, early!"

Skye and I walked out to the hearse, then drove a few blocks to The Kirkwood, a luxury apartment building near the square downtown.

"I feel like we're Sam and Dean from *Supernatural*," Skye said.

"Except our badges and IDs are real and this isn't a television show."

"We're also missing the cool car."

"The hearse is a *very* cool automobile," I said.

"Only you think so. To everyone else, it's the freak-mobile. This building looks old."

"It is. This used to be a hotel, but it was renovated into luxury apartments."

We walked inside to a reception area. The woman behind the desk stood. I reached into my vest pocket and pulled out my ID. Skye did the same.

"Hello Shirley," I said, reading her nametag. "I'm Special Agent Mulgrew. This is Agent Mackenzie. I believe you're expecting us. Could you show us to the crime scene please?"

"Certainly, follow me."

Shirley seemed nervous, perhaps because we were FBI agents, although I was taking some liberties calling us agents. We were investigators only, not agents, but I couldn't resist.

The elevator ride seemed long as we went to the top floor. Shirley led us down a hallway and unlocked a door for us.

"Thank you. We'll lock the door as we leave."

Skye and I stepped inside and closed the door.

"Agents?" Skye asked.

"Hey, I have to have some fun."

"Do you see anything?" Skye asked.

"No. If the victim stuck around she went elsewhere. There are no spirits in this apartment." I stood in the middle of the room and closed my eyes for several moments, then opened them.

"Anything? Skye asked.

"Nothing. Here's the chain the police had to break to get in," I said examining it. "There is no way this could have been locked from the outside and even a child couldn't slip through the space when the chain was fastened."

"I guess that rules out leprechaun attack."

"Very funny Skye."

"Did you see that movie? Those little bastards are vicious. I'm almost afraid to eat Lucky Charms now."

"O-k-a-y."

We walked to a sliding glass door that led out onto a very small balcony.

"Think anyone could climb up?" I asked, looking over the balcony to the ground far below.

"Yes, but it wouldn't be easy."

"I agree and since the sliding glass door was locked and can only be locked from the inside, I'd say no one came in or went

27

out this way. The windows were locked from the inside as well. The victim could have let her killer in, but if so how did he get out?"

Skye looked at the air vents.

"I thought of that, too small," I said.

"Unless she was murdered by a pygmy."

"Pygmy?" I asked.

"*Outer Limits*."

"I try to stick with the real world, Skye."

I gazed around the room looking for clues. I wasn't a detective and I sure wasn't Sherlock Holmes, but I wasn't looking for the kind of clue a detective such as Holmes would seek. I was looking for evidence of supernatural activity. The problem was, I came up with nothing.

"She was strangled with rope, except the cops didn't find any rope. Curiouser and curiouser. Search through the drawers, under the furniture and especially anywhere the cops and FBI might have missed."

"I think those guys are pretty thorough," Skye said. "If there was a rope in here they would have found it."

"Yes, but we're seeking something they weren't. Look for a small leather case, about the size of a wallet, but thinner. It wasn't listed on the inventory and it wasn't visible in any of the photos, but it should be here."

"What's so significant about it?"

"It's a Victorian calling card case and it was purchased in a local antique shop. A similar murder occurred in the apartment above the antique shop shortly before the murder here."

"Why would anyone be after a calling card case? Is it valuable?"

"Not especially, no. They're fairly common. In the 19th century people did a lot more visiting. If someone wasn't home, they left their card to show they had been there. A calling card is like a business card. They were even about the same size, but they usually only had the name of the individual who carried them. You search the left side of the apartment, I'll take the right."

"Should we be touching things? How about fingerprints?"

"They already dusted."

Skye and I set to work and methodically searched everywhere, even in the most unlikely places.

"Found something," Skye said a few minutes later, shining his flashlight under a dresser.

"The case?"

"No. The murder weapon."

"Don't touch it."

I quickly moved beside Skye.

"That I didn't expect to find. Let's move the dresser."

Skye and I stood, lifted the dresser, and moved it a few feet. Sitting on top of a layer of dust was a garrote. The rope looked very old.

"Why didn't the cops or the FBI find this? They couldn't have missed it," Skye said.

"Because it wasn't here when they searched."

"How is that possible?"

"We're dealing with the supernatural, Skye. Hmm, interesting. It shouldn't have been possible to remove the garrote from the victim's throat without untying the knots."

I pointed to a series of three knots and a closed off loop about the circumference of a human neck.

"In order to strangle a victim with this kind of garrote, it's necessary to loop the rope around the victim's neck, then tie the three knots, then put a stick or something similar between the outer two knots and turn. To get it back off, the murder would have to untie the knots or cut the rope."

"So, what did the killer do? Retie the knots after removing the garrote? What's the point? Why not leave it on the neck of the victim? Why go to the trouble of using a garrote at all? It would be easier to just strangle someone with a rope," Skye said.

"I don't know. Unless we're dealing with a spirit that can materialize the garrote around the victim's neck as he materializes."

"Is that possible?"

"Yes."

"So the victim didn't have a chance."

I shook my head.

"There is the possibility that the victim was incapacitated before the garrote was put around her neck. This is the same type of garrote John Gacy used. He convinced his victims to let him handcuff them and then killed them with a garrote."

I stood and called Agent Heck.

"Skye found something—the murder weapon."

Agent Heck was skeptical, but said he would send evidence technicians. I took photos of the garrote with my phone, then we departed, locking the apartment behind us. We took the elevator back to the ground floor.

"Technicians are coming to retrieve a piece of evidence we uncovered. Make sure no one goes in the apartment before they arrive," I told Shirley.

"Will this help you find Miss Shepard's killer?"

"We hope so," I said.

We departed and walked back to the car.

"I think Agent Heck will be glad he gave you a badge. You found something the FBI missed," I said.

Skye laughed.

"He saved me the trouble of picking one up at a toy store."

We headed back to campus, for it was nearing noon.

We entered the student union, which was called the IMU, which is short for Indiana Memorial Union, through the revolving door that led into the lobby of the Biddle Hotel. We turned toward the stairs, but I halted.

"What?" Skye asked.

"I'm waiting for the elderly gentlemen to come down."

"What elderly gentleman? Oh, never mind."

Skye knew I was seeing a ghost. I recognized him immediately. The specter was about eighty, rotund, and had a kind face. It was Herman Wells. He smiled and nodded at me as he passed. After he disappeared through the doors I looked up and noticed a huge painting hanging in the stairway.

"It was him," I said, pointing. "I saw him in the Rose Well House as well."

Skye and I walked up the first flight and gazed at the painting. The bronze tag read, "Herman Wells – President 1938-62 – Chancellor 1962-2000."

"Brendan knew him. He met him when he went to school here. I remember him telling me about him," I said.

"You'll have to tell him you met his old buddy."

I laughed. We continued on. When we arrived at the top of the stairs we had another surprise waiting on us. Colin was sitting on one of the couches in the East Lounge making out with a college girl.

Skye cleared his throat. Colin's eyes widened. I kept a straight face as Skye pulled out his ID and flashed his badge.

"Colin Stoffel. I'm afraid we'll have to ask you to come with us."

The girl's eyes widened as well.

Skye pulled Colin up by the arm.

"Good day, miss," he said.

We walked Colin out of the lounge and down the hallway.

"That was not cool! I suppose you think you're funny," Colin said.

I laughed.

"I knew this badge would come in useful," Skye said.

"I should report you to the FBI for misuse of your badge and harassing an innocent civilian."

"You're not that innocent and they would agree with me. That girl was too old for you."

"Oh, come on!"

"Did she know you're sixteen?"

"Well... I might have led her to believe I was college freshman."

"Uh huh. No more college girls, Colin."

"Grr, why couldn't you have stayed away for a few minutes longer?"

"Because it's my job to make sure you don't have any fun. Come on. We're taking you to lunch."

Colin forgave Skye quickly. We entered the Tudor Room and walked up to the podium. The hostess showed us to a table near one side of the room. The table was covered with a linen tablecloth. Our waiter, Alex, soon appeared. He was tall, slim, and quite handsome with his slightly long dark hair. I noticed Colin checking him out.

"What would you gentlemen like to drink? We have tea, coffee, and Coke products, as well as orange, apple, and cranberry juice."

Skye ordered cranberry juice, Colin a Coke, and I ordered iced tea.

"The main buffet is in the center or the room. On the far side is the soup and salad bar. The dessert bar is at the front and around the corner is the coffee and hot tea bar. Help yourselves. I will be back shortly with your drinks."

Skye went straight for the main buffet. Colin followed after checking out our waiter's butt. I hit the coffee and tea bar first so my tea would have time to brew. I picked up a tall clear glass stemmed cup and selected a jasmine green tea. I had never tried it before, but when I did a few minutes later I loved it. Ever since that day I've thought of that variety as "Tudor Room jasmine green tea."

I checked out the main buffet next. I selected chicken Kiev, herbed mashed potatoes, asparagus, and grilled tilapia, and then returned to the table where Skye and Colin were already eating.

I loved the Tudor Room. It was elegant with linen napkins and an upscale atmosphere, but not in the least stuffy. Some of the diners wore suits, while others wore sweat pants. The food was especially good and the service was excellent.

"How is wrestling?" I asked Colin. Skye, Colin, and I all lived in Graymoor Mansion, but Colin was a typical teenager, always busy, so I had few chances to talk to him.

"Great! I love it!"

"He's won every match so far," Skye said proudly.

"Well, I'd be scared if I walked out to the mat and you were there," I said.

Colin raised his arms up above his shoulders and flexed. His biceps bulged. A group of college girls sitting near checked him out. Colin noticed and grinned.

"You are way too much like your uncle," I said.

"There is no such thing as being too much like me," Skye said.

"Oh, believe me, there is."

"I'm going to try to break Skye's record this year. I came close my freshman year."

"You can do it. You're much tougher than Skye."

Colin grinned. Skye didn't challenge me. I'm sure he would like nothing better than to have Colin break his record. Skye had taken over raising Colin last year when Colin's mom and step dad were killed in an auto accident that nearly took Colin's life as well. Skye and Colin had always been close, but they were now even more so. They were close enough in age to be brothers, but they were like father and son.

"I miss wrestling...and football," Skye said.

"You just miss being the center of attention," I said.

"Ha! I am the center of attention wherever I go."

"Unless I'm with him." Colin grinned.

"Yeah, you are way too much like Skye. You have the same oversized ego."

"Oh, that's not the only thing that's oversized."

"Spare me the details."

Colin laughed.

We talked and ate while Colin flirted with girls at a nearby table. I was glad I wasn't sixteen. I was far more comfortable at twenty-four. Not having to deal with hormones was enough to make me appreciate being older. Adolescent males come close to being a different species. Believe me. I know. I used to be one.

Colin departed for more food and then Skye. I checked out the salad and soup bar and selected a small bowl of smoked Gouda potato soup.

"You don't eat much," Colin said when we were once again seated.

"He's not active like us. He's sedentary and doesn't require much food, sort of like a turtle," Skye said.

"I'm just not as obsessed with sports and working out as you two. I'm more intellectual."

"That's his way of telling us he's smarter than we are. He thinks we're too stupid to figure it out," Skye said.

"Well..." I grinned.

Later, we all hit the dessert bar. There were too many choices! There had to be at least a dozen different types of desserts and all of them looked scrumptious. I picked up a piece of cherry cheesecake and squeezed in a slice of chocolate cake beside it. Colin went for lemon and banana cream pie, while Skye had pecan pie with fresh strawberries and blueberries.

I had already finished my first cup of jasmine green tea and had another with my dessert. I contented myself with two desserts, but Skye returned for a no-bake cookie, and Colin went back for petit fours, apple pie with whipped cream, and a vanilla cup cake. We were all well stuffed by the time we finished.

"I need a nap," Colin said as we departed.

"Me too. Want to go for a run after?" Skye asked.

"Yeah."

"You two are sick," I said.

"You don't like naps?" Skye asked.

"Naps. Yes. Running? No. I only run if something is chasing me."

"I run a lot while I'm being chased... by girls," Colin said.

"Why am I not surprised?" I asked. Colin laughed. "I'm going to check out the second crime scene."

"Want me to come with you?" Skye asked.

"No, I've got this one. You two enjoy yourselves while I work, but don't feel guilty."

"What is this 'feel guilty' he speaks of?" Colin asked.

"It's some weird Marshall thing," Skye said.

I growled.

"I will come with you if you want. You did get me that sharp badge," Skye said.

"Which you used to ruin my fun!" Colin said. I guess he hadn't quite forgotten the incident.

"She was too old for you and it's my job to make sure you don't have fun."

"Well, you're doing an excellent job!"

"Thank you."

"I don't anticipate any trouble, but if you don't hear from me by four, come looking for me."

Skye and Colin went up to their room. I headed for the hearse and drove to Granny Bear's Antiques on the near west side. It did not take long to arrive. Nothing is very far away in Bloomington.

The bells rang as I entered the shop. It was filled with antique furniture, glassware, china, and toys, plus an odd assortment of scientific instruments, and even a real coffin.

"Can I help you?" asked an old lady of about eighty or so.

I flashed my ID and badge.

"I'm here to check over the crime scene."

"But the FBI was already here, as well as the local police."

"I'm a specialist."

"I hope you can find who did this. It's so horrible."

"We'll do our best."

"Here is a key to the apartment. It's the only door that is locked on the second floor. I have trouble making it up the stairs so I don't go up unless I must."

"Thank you. Oh, can you tell me anything about a Victorian calling card case you sold recently?"

"Let me think," she said, tapping her lower lip. "Oh yes. I sold it to that poor girl who was murdered. Two murders in less than a week! It's unheard of here."

"Can you describe it?"

"Well..." the old lady walked to a display cabinet and pulled out a small leather case. "It was a lot like this one, but plainer, without any tooling. It was also lighter in color and made of a strange leather."

"Strange how?"

"It was just different. I've been dealing in antiques for decades and have handled a lot of leather items. I don't know what animal hide it was made from, but it was unlike any of the other pieces I've had."

"Thank you."

I walked up the creaking stairs. The old building had seen better days.

I could feel a presence in the room even before I reached the door. Perhaps this time I could get some answers.

The door creaked open when I unlocked it to reveal a small room with a large bed, a dresser, and a bookcase filled with books along with other items of furniture. An elderly lady, or rather the ghost of one, who reminded me of the woman downstairs slowly rocked in a rocking chair in one corner of the room. She was far too old to be the ghost of the victim.

The ghost took no notice of me. She was likely one of those spirits who exist in their own world, seeing only what they wished to see. I felt a sense of contentment coming from her so I did not disturb her. I had hoped the presence I sensed was that of the victim, but no such luck.

I examined the room. A look out the windows revealed a fire escape. I tried each window. All had been painted shut in years past and there was no sign they had been opened. I knew the door was locked from the inside with a manual bolt when the body was discovered. The police had to bust it open to gain entrance, just as they did with the later crime scene. The furnace vents were even smaller than they were in the apartment Skye and I had checked out that morning. Again, the victim might have let her killer in, but there was no way for him to get back out.

I searched through the bookcase and the drawers of the dresser, but found nothing significant. The closet too revealed nothing unusual. I peered under the bed, but there wasn't so much as a dust bunny. There was nothing present that was out of the ordinary. I returned to the shop downstairs.

"Thank you," I said.

"I hope you get the murderer. Jill was such a kind woman. She worked in the shop part-time and we had become friends."

"She worked here? Was she working here the day the Victorian card case was sold?"

"Yes, she was. I remember well because she was murdered that night."

"Thank you for your help."

I stepped outside, walked to my car, and drove back to the hotel. Instead of going back to my room I walked around campus. I needed to think and I did my best thinking while I walked.

The murders had three things in common. Both occurred in rooms that were locked from the inside. Both were committed with the same, or at least the same type, of weapon. Both were connected to the Victorian card case. The first two common factors were the strongest. Even as an amateur, I was almost certain the same individual committed the murders. The card case was the weakest connection. The murder above the antique shop was committed after the case had been sold to the second victim. Not only was it not in the apartment above the shop at the time of the murder, it was no longer in the building. I was quite sure the FBI wouldn't consider it a significant factor, but they didn't hire me to conduct a standard investigation. I wasn't a detective and they had already investigated and turned up nothing. It was the weak link, but I was almost certain the card case was the key.

A large stream gurgled to the left of the path I followed. To the right was a large grassy area where college boys played touch football and Frisbee. It was October, but still pleasantly warm. I could see why so many of the Verona boys attended school here. The weather was much nicer than in northern Indiana.

I stopped in a small grove of enormous Cyprus trees and sat by the edge of the stream. What was so significant about the calling card case? Objects were often the cause of murders, but they were usually valuable objects. The card case wasn't rare or valuable. There were those who would kill for $10, but the real question was why would a ghost kill for it? Was a ghost the murderer or was it another supernatural entity? I had come across several different types of supernatural creatures in my lifetime, beings of legend that actually walked the earth. The problem with supernatural creatures is that it was often difficult to separate fact from fiction. Only by coming face-to-face with a supernatural being could I be sure its kind actually existed. Folklore often had it wrong. It was only a starting point that I used to get at the truth.

What if the culprit was not a ghost? Most supernatural creatures could no more depart from a room locked from the inside than a human. A changeling such as those mentioned in folklore might manage it by assuming a very small form, if a changeling was capable of transforming from something large enough to kill to something small enough to slip under the door, but since I had never run across a changeling I didn't know if they were fact or fiction. There were angels and numerous ancient gods that could appear at will, but I had not met any of the hundreds or perhaps thousands of gods that might possibly exist. A witch could perhaps kill from a distance, but again I had not met a witch. There were practicing witches, but they tended to employ herbs and white magic and could be considered a positive rather than a negative force. There was also voodoo, which might or might not be legitimate. When it came to the supernatural I believed nothing without proof, but dismissed nothing until it was disproven. I kept an open mind at all times.

We were staying the night in Bloomington and then heading out. I had checked out both crime scenes and it was time to move on. Now, it was time to ponder the case and do research. Most of my books were back in Graymoor Mansion, but I had brought along a small library of the titles I suspected might be useful and my laptop.

I remained by the stream for some time, thinking about the case and listening to the college boys play behind me. Soon, I felt the call of my computer. I returned to my room and set to work seeking a culprit and any possible significance of a Victorian calling card case.

I didn't realize how much time had passed when there was a knock on my door. I looked at the clock. It was 6:30.

"Are you getting hungry?" Skye asked.

"A little."

"I'm starved."

"After all you ate in the Tudor Room?"

"Yes! Let's go find Colin. We want to check out the bike shop too. Remember?"

"I had almost forgotten."

I joined Skye in the hallway. He was wearing jeans and a tight polo that strained to contain his chest and biceps. If I looked like him I'd be much more successful with women. The guys certainly flocked to Skye. He never lacked for hookups.

"Colin said he would stay in the building. He's probably hanging out in one of the lounges flirting with girls."

We wandered the hallways of the IMU for a few minutes, but didn't spot Colin.

"I'll text him," Skye said, pulling out his phone.

"No need," I said, grabbing his arm. We had just stepped into the South Lounge. Colin was sitting in a loveseat, making out with a college boy. Skye and I walked up to the pair, but they were oblivious to us. The college guy ran his hands all over Colin's chest.

"Colin Stoffel," Skye said.

Colin pulled back and turned to us.

"Oh crap. Not this again."

"What did I tell you earlier?"

"You said no more making out with college girls. In case you haven't noticed, Ben is a guy. You said nothing about older college guys."

"Bret," the boy corrected my nephew.

"Yeah, sorry Bret."

"He's got you there Skye" I said.

"Come on. We're going to eat," Skye said

"Sorry, I have to go. That's my uncle and he lives to make my life miserable."

"We all need a purpose," Skye said.

Colin stole another kiss before he joined us. I saw him mouth "text me" behind Skye's back. I grinned. Yeah, he was a younger version of Skye for sure.

"You are so unfair," Colin said as we walked through the hallway and past the Starbucks. "You hooked up with a college guy earlier this afternoon."

"Oh did he?" I asked.

"Yeah. He gave me twenty bucks to get lost." Colin grinned mischievously.

"You are sixteen. I am twenty-seven."

"Yeah, which means you're too old for college boys. An old man like you should stick to guys his age."

Colin laughed as Skye put him in a headlock.

"Old man. Huh?"

"Yeah!"

Colin laughed again. Skye released him.

We headed outside since we were walking this time. We exited the IMU to the south, entered the old part of campus, and followed the wide brick path on the northern edge of Dunn's Woods west to Indiana Avenue, which marked the boundary between campus and town. We crossed the street and walked down the sidewalk on Kirkwood. Just before we reached a small park we stopped.

"Here it is," said Skye.

"Here is what?" Colin asked.

"Peralta's Bike and Skate Shop."

The bell on the door rang as we entered. The owner, Marc Peralta, nodded and then recognized us.

"Skye and Marshall. Right?" he asked.

"Yeah, we met about a year ago at the Selby's Halloween wiener roast. Good memory. This is my nephew Colin," Skye said.

"It's nice to meet you, Colin."

"Nice shop," I said.

"Yeah, I started it a few years after I graduated. It's well known now. Everyone just calls it Peralta's."

I walked toward an old one-speed bike hanging on the wall beside a large trophy and a *Breaking Away* poster. There were also other photos; one was of a much younger Marc with three other boys his age, another was a signed photo of Marc with a blond guy.

"There's a bike race. Right? Casper told me about it. He said it's big deal," I said.

"Yeah. The Little 500. That's my bike that we used in the race my junior year at IU and beside it is the trophy we won. My frat, Alpha Alpha Omega let me have it after I coached the AAO team the first year."

"You won 1st Place?" Colin asked.

Marc grinned.

"Yes, by a fraction of a second."

"Who are the guys in the photos?" Skye asked.

"That's the team: Hunter, Conner, and Jonah. The guy in the other photo is Dennis Christopher. He played Dave Stoller in *Breaking Away*."

"Hey, that photo was taken in front of your shop," Colin said.

"Yeah, he was in town during Little 500 weekend and did an autograph signing here at the shop. It was great!

"Hey, how are Ethan & Nathan and Brendan & Casper and their boys?" Marc asked.

"They are all great," Skye said. "They come into the gymnasium to work out sometimes."

"Cool. I need to get back soon, but it's hard to get away. It's the downside to having my own business."

"Hey, we were going to grab something to eat. Want to come with us?" I asked.

"Sure. It's past closing time anyway." Marc smiled. He was very attractive for a guy who was probably forty or so.

"We were thinking about eating at Jimmy John's. We ate lunch at the Tudor Room so we aren't very hungry," I said.

"Speak for yourself," Skye and Colin said almost simultaneously.

"Oh, I love the Tudor Room. I eat there often. Jimmy John's is great and don't worry guys, they have big sandwiches."

Marc turned the sign to "Closed," shut off the lights, and locked up. We walked down the sidewalk. There was a big crowd across the street from the park and loud music coming from inside a building located just behind a large patio that was crowded with people.

"That's KOK," Marc said.

"Cock?" Colin asked, one eyebrow rising.

"K.O.K. Kilroy's on Kirkwood. It's a popular bar with the college crowd. The 'I Like KOK' tee-shirts are popular as well," Marc said.

"Oh, I need one to wear to school!" Colin said.

"No you don't!" Skye said.

"Hey, I have an idea. You guys go to Jimmy's Johns and I'll hang out in KOK," Colin said.

"No you won't," Skye said.

"They wouldn't let you in. You have to be twenty-one," Marc said.

Jimmy John's was located diagonally across from the small park and across the street from Kilroy's. It was quiet compared to KOK.

The restaurant was small, with only a few tables. It was done up in red, black, and white. A large menu was posted on the wall. We browsed until we each decided on a sandwich. Skye and Colin each ordered a J.J. Gargantuan and Marc a gourmet smoked ham club. I ordered a smaller sandwich, a J.J. B.L.T.

We got our drinks while we waited on our sandwiches and picked a table in a corner. Our sandwiches were ready almost as soon as we sat down.

"Holy crap!" I said when I noted the size of Skye and Colin's sandwiches. Gargantuan was right!

We caught Marc up on the happenings in Verona and he told us some of what was going on in Bloomington.

"It's too bad you guys aren't staying around. There is a football game this weekend. We are going to crush Purdue," Marc said.

"That would be cool," Colin said.

"Yeah, but we leave tomorrow," I said.

"That explains the 'Puck Furdue' tee-shirts I saw a few guys wearing earlier today," Skye said. Colin began to open his mouth, but Skye said, 'No" before he got the chance.

"Skye is here to make sure I have no fun at all," Colin said.

"You've had more than enough fun."

"Uh, no, but you could stay in Marshall's room tonight and I could..."

"Not happening."

"You aren't this uptight at home."

"There aren't tens of thousands of college kids around at home."

"Hey, I'm almost eighteen."

"Sorry, sixteen is not almost eighteen. It's sixteen, so no," Skye said. Colin growled, but he didn't seem too upset.

"You guys should come back when you have more time. There is always something to do here and lots of things to see."

"We're here on business. We're investigating the recent murders," I said.

"Really?"

"They are FBI agents," Colin said.

"Sort of... we're special investigators, more like consultants," I explained.

"Yeah, but they have badges and ID. Show him," Colin said.

Skye flipped out his FBI badge and ID and showed it to Marc.

"Wow."

"I had no idea you did that sort of thing," Marc said.

"It's a recent development."

"Now I feel boring," Marc said.

"Hardly, you own your own shop and you have a huge trophy on the wall. You sound successful to me," Skye said.

"I'm happy. That's the important thing. Back in school I wasn't sure what I was going to do, but then Hunter got me into biking. I had always loved skating. So, I came up with the idea of opening a shop and that decided my major. I graduated from the Kelly School of Business."

"I'm not sure what I want to do, unless Skye wants to retire and I take over his job," Colin said, grinning.

"Retire?" Skye said.

"Well, you are *really* old."

"Don't think I won't hurt you in front of witnesses."

Colin stuck out his tongue.

"You have time to make a decision. I started college clueless and remained that way through my freshman year. It was in my sophomore year that I figured things out," Marc said.

"I'm leaning toward porn star right now," Colin said.

"Oh good lord," Skye said. "This is why I don't often take him out in public."

Colin attempted to look innocent. His attempt failed.

"I'm glad I don't have kids," I said.

"Hey, I'm not a kid," Colin said.

"You know what I mean. I'm even gladder I don't have a teen. They're horrible!"

Colin laughed. "I bet Skye was worse at my age."

"Skye was worse than everyone at your age. It's a wonder your grandmother is sane," I said.

"Hey!" Skye said. "I was the perfect son."

"Yeah. Sure you were Skye."

"What did he do?"

"The things he did were so horrible I can't even tell you," I said.

"Marshall is full of crap," Skye said.

Marc laughed.

"You guys remind me of Brandon and Jon. I miss them," Marc said.

"Brendan has told us stories. They must have been hilarious," I said.

"They were."

"They aren't dead are they?" Colin asked.

"No, but they live far away, one in Florida, the other in North Dakota."

"North Dakota? That's worse than dead," Skye said.

"That would be near the bottom of my list of places to live as well. I'm too fond of warmth," Marc said. "That's one reason I love Bloomington. It's much warmer than Verona."

"Sure, rub it in," I said.

"I just plain love it here. It's not an especially large town, but it has everything most big cities have, except an IHOP. We need an IHOP. I rarely leave town. There is no reason to do so, except to come to Verona to visit Mom, Dad, and old friends."

"I like the college girls, and boys," Colin said.

"A little too much," Skye added.

"Hey, it was only making out!"

Marc raised an eyebrow. "You will have a great time in college," he said.

"That is the plan."

"Just don't do anything I did," Skye said, then laughed.

"Oh no. You are my inspiration."

"Uh oh."

We continued talking as we ate, then walked outside together. Music was still coming from KOK. We said goodbye to Marc, then walked past the bar and up Kirkwood onto campus. I kept catching glimpses of ghosts as we walked along, some in KOK and others strolling around the paths of IU. Bloomington was a very active place as far as supernatural activity was concerned, but most of it was benign.

We entered the IMU and walked up to our rooms, where we parted. I spent the rest of my evening and night doing research until I couldn't keep my eyes open. I gazed out my window over the campus. I could see why Marc liked Bloomington so much, but I was ready to head to our next destination. Perhaps we would discover something there that would help us crack a series of cases that left the professionals baffled.

Chapter Two

We packed up and headed out the next morning, after a trip downtown for breakfast at the Scholar's Inn Bakehouse. We drove away from Bloomington on winding roads that took us through the countryside and little towns. It was a pleasant trip, but slow going.

Our destination was the French Lick Resort, but we weren't on vacation. It had been kept quiet, but there had been a murder in the hotel a month earlier that was too similar to the Bloomington murders for coincidence.

French Lick was a very small town in the rolling hills of southern Indiana. It was much smaller than Bloomington and had little to offer except for two historic hotels and a casino.

"All right! A casino!" Colin said as we pulled up in front of the enormous hotel.

"Yes, which you are not allowed to enter," Skye said.

"Grr."

"I don't plan to gamble either, so don't complain," Skye said.

"Is there anything else to do here?"

"There is a pool, bowling alley, and a gym," I said.

"It won't be a total loss then."

We parked, grabbed our bags, and entered the lobby. The Biddle Hotel in Bloomington was beautiful, but the French Lick Hotel could best be described as grand. It had been restored and it was incredible.

"A lot of gangsters and movie stars used to stay here," I said.

"Really?"

"Yeah, stars like Clark Gable, John Barrymore, and Bob Hope."

"Who?"

"Sorry, I think he only knows 21st century celebrities," Skye said.

"Hey, I'm not elderly like you two."

"You sure you want to say that when we're sharing a room," Skye said.

"I'll take my chances. I actually do know who Clark Gable is. He once owned your Auburn."

"I miss my car," Skye said.

I grinned. Skye owned a 1935 Auburn boattail speedster that was purchased new by Clark Gable and later owned by James Dean. It cost a fortune and was Skye's prize possession.

"Don't worry, you two will be back together again soon and you can spend some quality time with your car," I said.

Skye sighed.

We checked in and took a long walk to our adjoining rooms, which were near the crime scene. The room where the murder had occurred was back in use so I didn't expect to find anything, but I hoped for a ghostly presence.

"We're only here for one night. Why don't you guys settle in and then we can check out the crime scene? I have the key."

"Well, if you have the key I could have my own room," Colin said.

"Do you really want to sleep alone in a room where a murder was committed?" Skye asked.

"I get your point. You can sleep there!"

"No."

"What's wrong? Scared Skye?" Colin asked.

"Yes, of what you would do in a room by yourself."

"I have my own room at home."

"It's hardly the same."

"True. Be afraid. Be very afraid."

I shook my head as Skye and Colin disappeared into their room.

The moment I walked into my room it was obvious it had been renovated. For one thing, it was too spacious to be the original floor plan. I had stayed in many old hotels and back in the late 19th and early 20th century the rooms were much smaller and often did not have their own bathroom. The original woodwork around the windows and doors had been preserved, adding an historic touch, but the rest was modern.

I settled in, made myself a cup of hot tea, and relaxed in an easy chair. I loved traveling with Skye and Colin, but it was nice to have some alone time. Of course, I was never quite alone. There was no presence in the room with me, but I had spotted a couple of ghosts on the way here. One was an elderly lady in 1920's attire who was completely unaware of the modern world.

Many ghosts were like that. They existed eternally in their own time. I didn't disturb those ghosts unless they were lost or in distress. The other ghost was a man in a suit who was likely from the 1960's, but it was hard to say because men's suits didn't change that much over time. He was aware of me, but concerned with his own business so I did not approach him. Many spirits needed help, but many did not.

I was eager to check out the crime scene, so after I finished my tea I stepped into the hallway and knocked on Skye's door.

"Ready?" I asked.

"Always. Want to come Colin?"

"Sure."

It probably was not wise to bring a sixteen-year-old along on a murder investigation, but Colin was not a typical boy of his age. I don't mean he possessed supernatural abilities, although he seemed more than usually sensitive to the presence of ghosts. Instead, I mean he was quite capable of taking care of himself. For months now he had been training with Skye and was a capable fighter. Of the three of us, I was the weakest link, not Colin.

I opened the door with the keycard and we stepped inside. The room was similar to mine and yet different. I was immediately disappointed because I hoped to find something there I had not at the other crime scenes—the specter of the victim. Once again, there was no sign of victim or murderer.

Skye and I checked under and behind furniture, but turned up nothing.

"Boy, I want to be an investigator for the FBI when I get older. This is so exciting I can hardly contain myself," Colin said with a smirk.

Skye playfully smacked him on the back of the head. Sometimes, Colin was a typical teenager.

We quickly wrapped up and exited the room.

"I'm going to head to the local police department and check out the evidence on hand. Why don't you guys enjoy yourselves?" I said.

"You sure you don't need us for backup? You could be in danger of nasty paper cut or you might drop a box on your toe," Colin said.

"I'd smack you if you weren't tougher than me."

Colin laughed.

"Let's meet about six for supper. Okay?" I asked.

The guys nodded. I headed for the parking lot and then drove my hearse the short distance to the police station in town. A few minutes later I was alone in a room sorting through a box that contained the contents of the hotel room the night of the murder. Two suitcases that contained only clothing had already been returned to the next of kin. I checked the inventory, but there was nothing in those suitcases of interest.

Inside the box were various papers, along with magazines, two books, and other miscellaneous items. The only item that stuck out was an 1885 edition of *Tom Sawyer*. It was notable because it was the only object in the box that was not modern and because it was missing it's cover. What's more, the cover had recently been torn off—very recently.

The title page immediately caught my interest because it was signed and inscribed, "To Belle, Happy Holidays, Samuel Clemens, December 22, 1885."

I paged through the rest of the book, but discovered nothing. There was no handwriting in the margins, no missing pages, and nothing out of the ordinary. The volume was in remarkably good shape for its age. It was not a first edition, but likely quite valuable if it was really signed by Samuel Clemens, a.k.a. Mark Twain, and I had no reason to doubt the signature. Why would someone intentionally ruin a book that obviously had value?

I took a photo of the inscription with my phone and placed the items back in the box. I had learned all I could here.

My cell rang as I pulled into a parking spot near the hotel. It was agent Beck.

"We have the report back on the garrote. It was definitely the murder weapon. The lab found DNA. traces from the last three murder victims as well as human D.N.A. from an individual who isn't in our database."

"The last three victims?"

"Yes. What's more, the rope is made out of hemp using a pattern that was common in the 19th century, but is little used now."

"So, the murderer used antique rope?"

"It looks like it, although we can't be sure. We're trying to get a date on it, but that will take time."

"That's odd. The only item missing from the last victim's apartment was a Victorian calling card case. I just examined the evidence from Alvin Pinckney's murder. There was one curious object in the box, a signed copy of *Tom Sawyer*. The cover had very recently been torn off. I'm trying to figure out why someone would ruin a valuable book. If it was the murderer, why steal the cover and not the entire book? It doesn't make sense."

"Do you think you're onto something?"

"I'm not sure yet, but it's all I've got at this point. None of the victims are earthbound so far."

I spoke with the agent a few more minutes, then headed inside. A pattern was emerging, but did it mean anything or was it mere coincidence?

I returned to my room and reviewed the information I had on the case, but there wasn't much more I could do. Mr. Pinckney had been killed under similar circumstances with the same murder weapon. His door was locked from the inside with a deadbolt and a chain the police had to break to gain entrance. The windows did not open. Once again, the murder could not be explained.

I gave my mind time to go over the information by walking through the old hotel. It was a mix of early 20th century splendor and the modern era. I found a display of photos of famous people who had visited including Franklin D. Roosevelt, Bing Crosby, and Abbott & Costello. It was too bad we couldn't travel here in Skye's car. The Auburn would have fit in nicely with the old hotel, but it only seated two.

I wandered into the newest addition, the casino. Before me was a sea of slot machines, all brightly lit. The casino was filled with gamblers and the dings and clicks of scores of slot machines in use. I had never been a gambler myself and the thought of sticking money in a machine did not appeal to me. If I spent a dollar, I wanted to know I was getting something for it. I could understand the appeal. The machines looked like fun and there was always the possibility of winning big. A new Ford pickup was on display, as well as a new Corvette and a Jeep. I wasn't tempted. I knew my odds of winning were slim.

I wandered through the hallways, admiring the ornate woodwork and artistic detail of the hotel. I stepped into the pool house and there I spotted Skye and Colin.

I would have given a million bucks to look like either of them, if I had a million that is, which I most assuredly did not. Skye was exceedingly handsome with his dark brown hair and brown eyes and his body was... flawless. He was muscular, without being too muscular and he was perfectly defined. If there was an illustration of the perfect male body in an encyclopedia it would've been a picture of Skye. He looked like a superhero, which wasn't that far from the truth. Skye had extraordinary abilities. Colin was a younger version of him. I identified as heterosexual, but I found them both beautiful.

I wasn't alone. Various members of both sexes of all ages were checking them out. The pair looked incredible fully clothed, but wearing only swimsuits... the sight of them was hard to describe.

"Marshall, put on a suit and join us," Colin said.

"Hey, I'm merely taking a walk. Don't try to pull me into physical activity."

"Playing in a pool hardly counts."

"It does for me!"

Colin grinned and shook his head.

I left the boys to their fun and continued my stroll around the hotel. The size of the place was impressive; especially considering it was built over a century before in the middle of nowhere. French Lick was a very small town and yet for decades thousands had come to visit. The casino was the big draw now, but in former years it was the health spa. The hotel was built because of the existence of a mineral spring. The water was marketed as Pluto Water, and I read on a display in one of the hallways that back in the day sales of the water often outpaced the profits from the hotel. From the description of the water, I was amazed. It smelled of sulfur and was basically ExLax in water form. It was supposed to cure all kinds of ailments, but I wondered if drinking it was worth the cure.

This was not the only hotel in French Lick either. The West Baden Hotel, located only a mile away, was just as old, just as large, and perhaps even more impressive.

I met Skye and Colin later for supper in the Powerplant Bar & Grill. The dining room was nice, without being too fancy. We were seated at a table near the wall that gave the restaurant its name. An enormous electrical switchboard that once powered the hotel took up nearly the entire wall.

After browsing the menus for a few minutes, Skye ordered a Cajun catfish sandwich, Colin the Buffalo Trace barbeque brisket, and I a crab cake sandwich.

The atmosphere was pleasant and the food quite good, but I found myself wishing we were back in Bloomington eating at the Tudor Room. Still, we had an enjoyable supper.

I enjoyed my time with Skye and Colin. I saw them often in Graymoor Mansion and had once spent weeks with Skye on a nearly unbelievable adventure, but the three of us rarely had a chance to sit and talk. Skye was too busy running the gymnasium and Natatorium at the mansion and Colin was too busy with school and wrestling. I had my own work and my constant research on the supernatural.

After supper, we went bowling. I was relieved that Skye and Colin were not expert bowlers. They still beat me, but at least they did not slaughter me as I had feared. When we tired of bowling, we bought ice cream cones and sat in rockers on the enormous front porch of the hotel.

"Where to tomorrow?" Skye asked.

"Oakland City, to speak with the widow of Alvin Pinckney."

"Is that in Indiana?" Colin asked.

"Yes."

"Sounds thrilling. Well, it's been nice hanging out with the old folks here at the rest home, but there are some girls who wanted to spend time with me. I promised to meet them," Colin said.

"How old are these girls?" Skye asked.

"They're like... twenty-five, maybe thirty. I think one has a kid in grade school."

"Seriously?" I asked.

"You are too gullible Marshall."

"One of these days Colin," I said, punching my palm with my fist. Colin laughed.

"They're my age."

"Stay out of trouble and be back in the room by eleven at the latest," Skye said.

"Yes Father."

I laughed as Colin departed.

"I couldn't interest you in a sixteen-year-old could I?" Skye asked me.

"Do I look stupid?" Skye started to open his mouth. "Wait! Don't answer that, but no. I prefer to deal with the dead. It's easier."

"It probably is and Colin is a great kid. I'd be pulling my hair out if he was a trouble-maker."

"You'd better enjoy your time with him. Before you know it he'll be off to college."

"Yeah. I know. I do enjoy my time with him. I never thought I'd have a son, but I think of Colin as mine."

"Your sister would be very proud of how well you've done with him."

"I hope so. I miss her."

"I can't think of anyone better to raise him."

"Thanks."

Us old folks in our twenties remained on the porch for a while longer then went in. Skye wandered off somewhere. I returned to my room to do more research on the cases we were investigating. We had made little progress and yet I was certain we were on to something.

Chapter Three

"This isn't Oakland City," Skye said as we passed a sign that read, *Welcome to Blackford, Indiana.*

"Very good Skye. And they say jocks are dumb," I taunted.

"Thank you, smart ass. Why are we here?"

"I love to hear you guys bicker. How long have you been married?" Colin asked.

Skye growled.

"We have a case to check out in town and Oakland City isn't that far."

"Where are we staying?"

"You'll see."

"Is there anything to do in this town? Please tell me there is something to do. It looks about the size of Verona," Colin said.

"There is a theatre, an ice cream shop, and an antique store."

"In other words, no. In Verona at least I could hang out with my friends."

"They'll still be there when we get back. You better enjoy being out of school. Your fall break is quickly coming to an end," Skye said.

"Don't remind me, although I am eager to get back to wrestling practices."

"Sicko," I said. Colin laughed.

We entered town. At first we passed only homes, but soon we entered the downtown area. There was no square, but there were a surprising number of businesses. We passed the Delphi Theatre, Merton's Ice Cream Parlor, and a Marathon station, to name a few.

"Hey Colin, if you miss school I can let you out," I said as I stopped at the stop sign. Directly ahead was the Blackford High School.

"Thanks, but I'll pass."

I made a couple of turns and drove to the southern edge of town. We passed an A&W Root Beer drive-in that looked like it belonged in the 1950's and then we were out of town. We passed two farms and kept on going.

"Uh, Marshall..." Skye said.

I turned into a long winding drive and headed through a small forest.

"Where *are* you taking us? Colin asked.

"Skye knows."

"I don't think he'll be happy if we just drop in. Besides, he's probably out on a book tour."

"We are expected," Marshall said.

"You might have told me!"

"And ruin the surprise?"

We pulled up in front of a large brick 19th century farmhouse. It was probably over 150 years old, but had been fully restored.

"Grab your bags," I said.

We walked up onto the porch and knocked. In only a minute or so Thad opened the door. Thad T. Thomas was a writer of supernatural novels who had often stayed in Graymoor Mansion. He even featured the mansion in one of his books. Skye had been rather infatuated with him at one time and Thad was the only guy Skye had ever failed to seduce. Still, they were good friends.

"Come on in. I'll show you to your rooms and then we'll talk. I want to hear all about this case of yours," Thad said.

We followed Thad upstairs.

"The first two rooms on the left are my study and bedroom, but you can use any of the others you wish. Just pick out one you like."

"I get my own room?" Colin asked.

"Of course. I'm not cruel enough to ask you to room with Skye."

Colin laughed.

"I like you already. I'm Colin, Skye's nephew."

"I can see the resemblance. Please tell me you're not too much like him."

"Only a little."

"Hey, no ganging up on me," Skye said.

"You're a big boy. You can handle it," Thad said.

Thad waited while we dropped our bags in our rooms. Mine was furnished in the Eastlake style, a lighter style of Victorian than my room in the Graymoor Mansion. There was a matching oak bed, dresser, and washstand. There was an old painting of a handsome boy in a gilt frame on one wall. I took a closer look. I recognized the boy, Josiah Huntington. He had lived for a time in Graymoor Mansion and was a friend of Thad's.

I returned to the hall. We followed Thad back downstairs and into the kitchen. It was furnished and decorated with antiques, but was a decidedly masculine kitchen. Thad put on a kettle as the rest of us took seats around the oak table.

"Would anyone prefer coffee? I also have Coke and root beer."

"I'd like a Coke," Colin said.

Thad filled a glass with ice and got Colin a Coke from the refrigerator.

"If you want more, help yourself. So, how have you guys been?"

"The usual, ghosts, hauntings, alleged possession, and poltergeists," I said.

Thad smiled one of his barely-a-smile smiles.

"You do have an interesting life Marshall. How about you Skye?"

"Work keeps me busy and so does this guy," he said, pointing to Colin, who did his best to look innocent.

"I bet *you* have take care of *him*," Thad said to Colin.

"Constantly. Trying to keep him out of trouble is exhausting."

Skye crossed his arms and glared.

"So tell me about this case," Thad said.

I summarized what we had discovered so far. I was eager to get Thad's take on it. Thad was quite acquainted with the supernatural. It was his genre and he had extensive experience.

"You're dealing with either a vengeful spirit or a minor god. There is no question about it."

"A god?" Colin asked.

"There are hundreds of them, perhaps thousands. The ancient Celts believed a spirit inhabited every tree and spring. Most dismiss it as nonsense, but the Celts were right. There are a lot of pissed off nature spirits out there, but this is a step above. This isn't an ordinary spirit."

"I've focused on the method used, but can't find anything significant about the use of a garrote. It was the preferred murder weapon of a handful of serial killers and was used as a means of execution by some past civilizations, but it isn't the trademark of any.

"The closest link I found is of John Wayne Gacy, a serial killer who murdered at least 33 boys and young men, but even he didn't always use a garrote. He was executed in 1994, but I don't think we're dealing with his spirit."

"I agree, the victims don't match his profile. If his spirit came back to continue his murder spree it wouldn't be after women or older men," Thad said.

"Exactly."

The kettle whistled and Thad made us Yorkshire tea.

"You're on the right track, Marshall. The missing objects are the key."

"But why the hell would anyone steal a card case they could probably pick up at most antique malls for $10? The book cover makes even less sense. I could see taking the entire book because it had value, but why rip off the cover and take only it?" Skye asked.

"That's why the case and the book cover are the focus of the investigation. It makes sense to the murderer," Thad said.

"Maybe the murderer is just plain crazy," Colin said.

"Madness is a possibility," Marshall said.

"As you look at more cases, focus on whatever item or items are missing and figure out what they have in common," Thad said.

"So far, the only common factor is that both items are from the 19th century," Marshall said.

"That is no doubt significant, but you need more data. Do you know if the book's cover was cloth or leather?"

"It should have been cloth. I looked it up online and nearly all of Twain's works were published with cloth covers."

"There isn't much of a connection then. The objects are similar in age, but I don't see that they have anything else in common."

"Except that they are nearly worthless," Skye said.

"Yes, to us, but not to the murderer," Thad said.

"Hey, I need to head to Oakland City to question the widow of one of the victims. Do you mind babysitting for me Thad?" I asked.

"Hey!" Skye and Colin said simultaneously.

"No, I'm accustomed to babysitting with this one," Thad said, pointing to Skye. "It will be easier this time since I have Colin to help."

"We should have stayed in a hotel," Skye said.

"I'll be nice. Well, nice for me," Thad said.

"That's not that nice," Skye said.

Colin smiled as he watched the interchange between Thad and his uncle. I wondered if Skye had ever told him he was once, and perhaps still is, romantically interested in the older writer.

"Well, I'm heading out. I'll be back later."

"Want me to come along?" Skye asked.

"No, I've got this one. I thought you and Thad would like to visit."

I set out for Oakland City. Despite his grumbling, I knew Skye was glad to see Thad again. There was a time I thought Skye might actually settle down with Thad, but it didn't happen. Since then, Skye had met someone else, someone perfect for him, but sadly they could not be together. Skye's life looked like a dream from the outside, but it was no truer for him than anyone else. The weight on his shoulders was considerably greater than it was for most, but he always seemed to keep a positive attitude.

The drive to Oakland City was pleasant. I followed a country highway through the autumn foliage. Many of the leaves had already fallen in Verona, but they were in their full glory in southern Indiana.

In a little less than an hour, I reached Oakland City. There wasn't that much to see. I spotted an IGA before I turned onto Main Street, but Main itself had little to offer. There were several empty buildings and grassy lots that indicated where businesses had been, but only a few stores were in operation. Oakland City was obviously well past its heyday. Gazing at it, I realized how lucky we were that Verona was still a thriving community.

I found the residence of Mrs. Pinckney without difficulty near the outskirts of town. She lived in a small, but well kept home in a pleasant residential area. I walked up to the door and knocked.

"I'm Agent Mulgrew. I hate to bother you, but I'd like to ask you a few questions," I said, showing her my badge and ID.

Mrs. Pinckney hesitated, but then let me in.

"I've already spoken to the police."

"My investigation is following a different line. I actually have only one main question. Among the items left in your husband's room was a book, a signed copy of *Tom Sawyer*. What can you tell me about it?"

"He was very excited about obtaining that volume, so excited he took it with him. Alvin liked to play the slots. He wasn't a serious gambler, mind you. He only took what he was willing to lose. About once a month, he went to French Lick to stay overnight and play the slots. I don't care for gambling, so while he's gone I usually stayed with my sister. Alvin always came back with a little something he bought for me, only last time he didn't come back."

Mrs. Pinckney's eyes watered.

"Was the book missing its cover when he purchased it?"

"No. Are you saying it is now?"

"I'm afraid so. The cover was ripped off and it's not among your husband's belongings."

"That's a shame. I was looking forward to getting that back. I thought I would give it to our grandson."

"The rest of the book is intact. I'm sure he would like to have the inscription and signature of Samuel Clemens. Do you know where your husband purchased the book?"

"Yes, he purchased it at an online auction."

"eBay?"

"No, it was another auction company. They were liquidating a large library."

"Do you know what it is called?"

"Yes, Live Auctioneers or something similar. My husband was always browsing there."

"Thank you. This could be very helpful."

Mrs. Pinckney looked skeptical.

"It's often small, seemingly insignificant details that are the key to a case," I said.

"I don't see how anyone can solve this one."

"It is perplexing, but every case can be solved and I believe I'm getting closer. I intend to find who did this and stop them from doing it again."

Mrs. Pinckney smiled sadly.

"Can you tell me about the cover of the book? Was it cloth?"

"It was leather. My husband would have preferred it to be cloth since it was originally issued with a cloth cover, but he purchased it because of the inscription and signature."

"What color was the leather?"

"It was light, unusually light."

"I think that's all I need. I'm sorry for troubling you and thank you for your time."

Mrs. Pinckney escorted me out. I was soon on my way back to Blackford.

I didn't see Thad, Skye, or Colin when I returned so I headed straight to my room. I opened up my laptop and searched for the auction company. It took only seconds to find their site. A search for 'Samuel Clemens signed book' turned up only three entries. Only one of the volumes was a signed edition of *Tom Sawyer*.

I clicked on the link and read the description; "Rebound, 1885 edition of Tom Sawyer inscribed and signed by Samuel Clemens. Condition: no tears, no missing pages, and only minimal foxing."

I was almost certain I found the book. I clicked on the thumbnail of the title page. I pulled out my cell phone and opened the photo I had taken. The inscription and signature was an exact match. This was the volume purchased by Alvin Pinckney.

I clicked on the thumbnail of a photo that showed that binding. The volume had been rebound as indicated in the description.

I looked closely at the photos of the cover and spine. The leather was very light in color and had an unusual texture. I recalled what the antique dealer had told me about the Victorian calling card case. She said it was made of an unusual leather, very light in color that she could not identify.

"You're back. I didn't hear you come in."

I turned. Thad stood in the doorway. "Yes, and I think I found another connection between the murders."

I described my discovery and showed Thad the photos of the book. He peered closely at the cover and spine of the book.

"I've seen leather like this before, but... I can't remember, but I know I've seen it." Thad shook his head. "Perhaps it will come to me later."

"Where are Skye and Colin?"

"They discovered I have a weight machine so..."

"Say no more. They're fitness freaks. I'm afraid it's incurable."

"How is Skye?" Thad asked.

"He's doing well, all things considered. Losing his sister was hard on him, but Colin keeps him busy. They're very good for each other."

"I had a hard time picturing Skye as a father when I heard the news, but they seem to have a good relationship."

"Skye has done a remarkable job with Colin. Losing his mom was difficult for Colin, but he's emotionally strong. I think he helps Skye as much as Skye helps him."

"They're probably both starving now so I thought we could drive into town and get something to eat."

"That sounds good to me."

I quickly saved photos of the book cover and then powered down my laptop. Thad led me to Skye and Colin in a workout room downstairs.

"Nice. If you like this sort of thing," I said.

There was a weight machine, an exercise bike, dumbbells, and a big screen TV.

"After I've been writing all day I want to do something physical," Thad said.

"Well..." Skye began.

"Don't go there."

Colin laughed. "Shot down!"

"Hey!" Skye said.

"We are going out to eat. Would you like to join us or continue with the self-torment?" I asked.

"Let's eat!" Colin said.

"I can drive, but someone will have to ride in the back," I said.

"I will. Have any flowers I can hold?" Colin asked.

Thad looked confused.

"Marshall drives a hearse, which I'm sure comes as no great shock," Skye said.

"I can't say I'm surprised," Thad said.

We walked out to the car. Colin climbed in the back and stretched out.

"You need a mattress back here," he said.

"Really? No one has ever complained before," I said.

"Probably because they were dead."

"A casket would be comfortable. If you had one Colin could ride in it and then we could make a drop off at the cemetery," Skye said.

"Not funny!"

I drove into town. Thad directed me to the downtown area where we parked near The Black Heifer Diner.

"The Black Heifer? Seriously? I didn't think there was a place more backward than Verona, but I was wrong," Colin said.

"Wait until you taste the food," Thad said.

Most of the tables were filled, which was always a good sign. The clientele ranged from farmers to teens to old ladies to businessmen. The décor was farm and cattle based. There were photos of all different types of cattle on the walls. On a ledge an antique milk can, milk bottles, dairy advertising, and other nostalgic items were displayed.

"The burgers here are great, but the breakfasts are even better and are served all day," Thad said.

We browsed the menus until a waitress took our drink orders, then went back to the difficult task of deciding. I was tempted by the breakfasts, but decided to try the bison burger. It had been a long time since I'd had one and the Black Heifer version came with lettuce, tomato, onion, and three cheeses.

The waitress soon returned with my Coke and the other drinks. Skye and Colin both ordered the Hungry Heifer, which was a breakfast platter. Thad ordered a barbecue bacon burger.

I filled Skye and Colin in on my progress while we waited on our food.

"I thought this investigation would be more exciting," Colin said.

"The excitement comes later," I said.

"When?"

"That's the question, but believe me, before the end there will likely be enough danger and excitement for everyone."

"Yeah, but I'll probably be stuck in school."

"You never know."

Our orders arrived a few minutes later. The burgers were extra-large and came with a mound of fries, but the Hungry Heifer platters were enormous. It took two waitresses two trips to bring everything. Thad and I gave up most of our table space to Skye and Colin's plates and platters of pancakes, scrambled eggs, biscuits & gravy, hash browns, sausage links, and bacon. I simply stared.

"What no muffins or eggs benedict?" I asked.

"We're eating light today," Colin said.

"And saving room for dessert," Skye added.

I knew for a fact that neither Colin nor Skye usually ate so much.

"There is no way you can finish that," I said.

"Twenty bucks says I can," Colin said.

"It's a bet." Colin and I shook hands.

"Contributing to the delinquency of a minor I see," Skye said.

"Hey, he made the offer."

"Yeah, I'm contributing to the delinquency of an adult," Colin said.

We talked little while we ate. My burger was incredible. I didn't think I could eat it all when I started, but it was so good I did. Even the fries tasted extra delicious.

Skye and Colin slowly worked their way through their enormous breakfasts. Their plates slowly emptied. Skye quit before he quite finished everything, but he ate most of it. Colin was still eating when the rest of us were done.

"I'll let you out of the bet for $10 right now just so you won't hurl," I said.

"Ha! You're scared. You might as well pull that Andrew Jackson out of your wallet because it is mine!"

Skye, Thad, and I talked while Colin ate. A few minutes later Colin pushed the last empty plate away.

"Are we getting dessert?" he asked, then laughed.

"That's impressive," Thad said.

Colin grinned at me.

"Pay up loser!"

I pulled out my wallet and handed Colin a twenty. We paid the check and walked outside.

"Come down the street, I want to show you Angel and Kurt's theatre," Thad said.

"Who are Angel and Kurt?" Colin asked.

"My dads."

Thad walked on without explaining, which was not a surprise. Thad wasn't big on explanations and was secretive about his early years. I often suspected there was more to him than there appeared to be, but what the more was I did not know.

It was half past seven, but night had already come. The flashing lights of the marquee chased away the darkness. Above the marquee, neon letters three feet high spelled out Delphi. From the outside, the theatre looked as it must have back in the 1920's. I loved old theatres. They were quite often haunted.

The boy in the ticket booth waved at Thad as he led us past and inside. The show had started at seven. I could hear bits of it through the auditorium doors, but we hadn't come to watch *Transformers*.

The lobby was art deco with dark crimson carpet and a black and white marble floor. A massive chandelier dominated the space, but there were touches of elegance everywhere. Art deco sconces and mirrors brightened the walls and there was crimson and gold everywhere. Movie posters in large, ornate frames advertised coming attractions.

The ceiling was decorated with gilded cherubs, horses, and chariots. Even the concession stand was beautiful with its marble counter and antique glass display cases. I felt as if I had stepped back in time.

Angel smiled when he spotted us and quickly crossed the lobby to greet us. Angel was close to seventy, but looked much

63

younger. He wore his hair in a long ponytail, which suited him perfectly.

"What brings you to Blackford?" he asked.

"We're working on a case, one in my area," I said, since I did not want the few others who were around to overhear too much.

"Ah, I see. It's nice to see you again Marshall and you, too, Skye. Who is this young man?"

"I'm Colin. I'm Skye's nephew."

"I can see the resemblance. Kurt! Look who is here!"

Kurt was the same age as Angel and like him looked younger. Kurt was somewhat shorter than Angel and unlike him wore his hair short. Kurt shook all our hands.

"Thad didn't tell us you were coming," Kurt said.

"You know Thad, he's not big on sharing information," Skye said. Thad's eyes flashed and Skye grinned.

"Well, I'm glad you're here in any case. How do you like the theatre?"

"It's beautiful. You restored all this. Right?" I asked.

"We oversaw the restoration. It was a mess when we purchased it and in danger of being torn down. Luckily, the structure was sound and we were able to purchase it before it was too far gone. It closed around 1980 and sat empty for over two decades. We only opened it back up a couple of years ago."

"We had far too many memories of this place to let it go to ruin," Angel said. "So did many others in town. People are constantly coming up to us and telling us how they had their first date here or used to work the concession stand when they were a kid. Half the residents of Blackford had their first kiss here. I doubt we will ever come out ahead on our investment, but bringing the Delphi back to life was never about money."

"This is so much cooler than the multiplexes in South Bend," Colin said.

"It would be nice to restore the Paramount in Verona, but at least it is in no danger of being torn down," I said.

"Once a month we have a "Blast from the Past" night that focuses on a different decade or event. The last was a 1950's night. We showed *Singin' in the Rain* and everything from admission to concessions were 1950's prices. People are encouraged to come in costume and there is often something else going on in town that links up with the theme. For 1950's night the P.T.A. sponsored a car show focusing on automobiles from that decade. There were so many '57 Chevy's and other cars from that era in town it looked as if it was the '50s again," Angel said.

Angel and Kurt gave us a tour. While I listened and admired the old theatre I focused on the spirits I spotted here. There was the ghost of an usher who kept an eye on the lobby and disappeared into the auditorium from time to time. I saw a couple rushing in late to the show. They looked as if they were here for 1950's night, but instead they were from the 1950's themselves. I felt sad for those who could not see what was all around them, but perhaps it was best. It could be a bit disorientating at times.

After our tour and a short visit, we returned to Thad's house where he lit a fire in a downstairs parlor. We sat around talking while Colin roasted marshmallows in the fireplace.

"How can you possibly still be hungry?" I asked.

"I can always eat. Want to bet I can finish this entire bag of marshmallows?"

"Oh no. You aren't suckering me in again."

Colin laughed.

"What's up next for you?" Thad asked me.

"We have a case to check out here in town."

"The bank vault suicide," Thad said.

I nodded.

"Bank vault suicide?" Skye asked.

"It's been all anyone can talk about in town for weeks. The local bank manager was found strangled to death inside the vault. It was reported as a suicide, except..."

"...no one can figure out how he did it," I finished.

"Exactly. Most people believe he hung himself with his tie, ignoring the fact he was wearing it when he was found and it was properly in place," Thad said.

"People come up with a lot of illogical explanations when they come up against something they don't understand," I said.

"He died while alone in a locked vault. The idea that he suffocated from lack of oxygen was brought up first, but then it was pointed out there is more than enough breathable air inside for one person for far longer than he was in there," Thad said.

"So, we're checking it out," I said.

"You don't think it was suicide. Do you?" Skye asked.

"I know it wasn't. He was murdered. I've looked at the crime scene photos and read the autopsy report. The victim was strangled and not with his own tie."

"He was murdered while alone, inside a locked bank vault. So, who you gonna call?" Skye asked mischievously.

"I'm going to hurt you if you do any more *Ghostbusters* references," I said.

"What's *Ghostbusters*? Is that one of those old films you like Skye?" Colin asked.

"*Ghostbusters* isn't that old. It came out around 1984, I think."

"Oh my god! That's ancient! Is it a silent film?"

"Come closer so I can hurt you."

Colin laughed.

We stayed by the fire talking until late. I considering doing a little more research, but it was pointless. I had done all I could for now. Hopefully, I would turn up some useful information tomorrow.

***

Marshall and I walked to the bank the next morning after we had breakfast with Colin at the Blackford Café. Colin wasn't interested in joining us. Instead, he headed for the park where he hoped to join a basketball or football game. We reminded him we were meeting Thad at the Black Heifer at noon for lunch.

A teller directed us to the new bank manager, Mr. Proffit, who showed us the vault.

"Could anyone have opened the vault while Mr. Beakman was inside?" I asked.

"I'm the only other person who knows the combination to the safe and even I could not have opened it. Once the vault is locked any time after 5 p.m., it cannot be opened again until 8 a.m. the next morning. The vault has a timing mechanism. The only way to get in would be to cut through the door."

"Show us the surveillance tape," I said.

The manager led us into his office, where he retrieved the tape from a locked cabinet.

"We close at 6 p.m. This tape begins shortly before that. Mr. Beakman entered the vault at 6:18 p.m."

We sat and watched the tape. A few last customers departed and then the guard locked the door from the inside at 6 p.m. The tellers finished up their work and deposited their drawers inside the vault. The guard let them out as they each finished for the day. I momentarily caught sight of Mr. Beakman as he bid one of the tellers goodbye. The last to leave were Mr. Proffit and the guard, who departed together. The guard locked the doors from the outside, leaving only Mr. Beakman in the bank.

The cameras showed Mr. Beakman making rounds inside the bank, checking to see that was all well. He turned off the lights in his office and closed the door. He walked to the safe and then things got interesting.

Mr. Beakman jerked around as if someone had surprised him, but no one was visible on the tape. He screamed as an expression of sheer terror altered his features. He dashed into the vault, pulling the door shut after him. Mr. Proffit paused the tape.

"I want you to watch what happens next carefully. It should not be possible for anyone to lock themselves in the safe."

"So, merely closing the door doesn't lock the safe?" I asked.

"No. The handle must be turned and that can only be done from the outside."

Mr. Proffit started the tape again. The three of us watched as the spoked handle turned by itself. The tape continued, but there was no sign of anyone in the interior of the bank.

"I can't explain it. I can't believe Mr. Beakman killed himself. He had no reason to do so and showed no signs of distress. He was happy, well-adjusted, and friendly with all the employees. It seems impossible that he killed himself, but..." Mr. Proffit trailed off.

"Did Mr. Beakman collect anything?" I asked.

"Collect anything?"

"Yes, like antiques, especially anything from the 19th century or anything leather."

Mr. Proffit looked thoroughly confused, as well he might.

"No, but he did have an antique wallet that belonged to his great-grandfather I believe. He always carried it with him inside the jacket of his suit."

"Was it found on him when his body was discovered?" Skye asked.

"I... don't know."

"Well, thank you for your time, Mr. Proffit. You have been most helpful," I said.

"I don't see how, but I wish we could get to the bottom of this."

"That's what we're trying to do."

"I can't understand why he would kill himself or what frightened him so. Is it possible to be scared to death?"

"It is, but that's not what happened with Mr. Beakman."

Mr. Proffit eyed me.

"You don't think he killed himself either, do you?"

I shook my head.

"But how..."

"That's what we intend to find out."

We hurried back to Thad's house, where I went through the file on the Beakman case. I checked the inventory. There was no wallet, other than the one he carried in his back pocket that continued his cash and credit cards. I looked at the time. I had an hour before noon. I wrote down the address of Mr. Beakman's widow, grabbed Skye, and headed back into town.

We drove to the Beakman home on the outskirts of Blackford. It was a two-story brick Victorian with white wooden shutters. We walked up the brick pathway and knocked on the front door.

"Mrs. Beakman? I'm Agent Mulgrew. This is Agent Mackenzie. We hate to bother you, but we have a few questions. It won't take long. I promise."

Mrs. Beakman escorted us into a clean, modern living room where we all took seats.

"Your husband owned an antique wallet. Did he take that wallet with him on August 4th?"

"I don't know, but I'm sure he did. He kept it in his suit pocket. It was a family heirloom. I don't think it was especially valuable, but it had a lot of sentimental value for him. You know? His father carried it until the day he died."

"Was the wallet returned to you in his effects?"

"No. It wasn't. I hadn't really thought of that before. Odd."

"Can you describe it?"

"It was a leather wallet, quite plain, scuffed, and worn. It wasn't the most attractive thing, but then I rarely saw it. It was about the size of a checkbook cover, maybe a little wider."

"What shade was the leather?"

"Light, unusually light. My husband thought it was perhaps made of buckskin."

"Thank you. I think that will be all."

We left Mrs. Beakman as confused as Mr. Proffit, but we had another piece to the puzzle.

Thad and Colin were already seated in a booth in the Black Heifer when we arrived. Colin grinned at Skye evilly.

"What?" Skye asked suspiciously.

"Nothing. Thad and I have been exchanging information."

"What information?"

"You'll never know. Ba-ha-ha."

"Are you corrupting my nephew?" Skye asked Thad.

"I'm not corrupting him. I'm enlightening him."

"Why does the two of you together make me uneasy?" Skye asked.

"Because you're not as dumb as you look?" I suggested.

"Grr."

"So, what did you discover?" Thad asked.

"The suicide was definitely not a suicide. The victim had no reason to be suicidal. He was strangled inside a locked vault that was locked with a time lock. Even someone with the combination could not have entered. The only object the victim could have used to kill himself was his tie, which was neatly and properly tied around his neck.

"The most significant detail is that a single object is missing; it was not on the victim when his body was discovered and he always kept it in the coat pocket of his suit. Want to guess what it was made of?"

69

"Leather," Thad said.

"Exactly. Not only that, but it was an unusual leather, light in color that the victim's widow thinks might have been buckskin."

Thad looked thoughtful.

"I've seen buckskin. It tends to be light in color, but I don't think the book cover was buckskin. It was something...stranger," he said.

"Buckskin was merely the victim's guess, although it was a good guess. The item missing is a 19th century wallet, which could well be made from buckskin. It was in far more common use then than now," I said.

"Yeah. Yeah. Let's order," Colin said.

"Will you be having the feeding frenzy again?" I asked.

Colin laughed. "Yeah. I'm ordering the Hungry Heifer, but I think feeding frenzy is a better name for it."

"I think I'll just have blueberry pancakes and bacon this time," Skye said. "Maybe with some scrambled eggs and French toast."

I rolled my eyes.

We ordered.

"So where are you headed next?" Thad said.

"Back to Verona. It's time for some serious research and Colin has school."

"Hey, I thought we agreed not to mention the s-word," Colin said.

"What are you up to Thad?" I asked.

"Writing. What else?"

"Don't let him fool you. He's a slacker. He just changes the names in one of his old books, gives it a new title, and publishes it. He doesn't actually do anything," Skye said.

"Says the man who plays with weight equipment and lounges around a pool and calls it work," Thad said.

Colin laughed.

Our food arrived soon. I ordered breakfast myself this time, but not the Hungry Heifer. I had eggs benedict and raspberry and pecan pancakes, which was more than enough for me.

"Do you have a regular schedule for writing or do you write when the mood hits you?" I asked Thad.

"I maintain a fairly regular schedule. I do first drafts in the mornings. After lunch I work on revisions and all the non-writing work that comes with being a writer. I usually like to get my work out of the way and then have leisure time. I rarely come out for lunch like this, but I'll make it up by putting in a little extra time this afternoon."

"I'm amazed at anyone who can write or do anything artistic."

"I'm in awe of those who can see the dead. The things I could write if I had that ability..."

"Please, no mutual admiration society," Skye said.

"I don't get how you can sit down and just...write," I said.

Thad smiled. "Well, I begin with an idea and then add to it. The first draft is the hardest. Hemingway said that writing a first draft is like passing a kidney stone the size of a brick and he wasn't far off. It's difficult for me to focus on a first draft, but later drafts are much easier and more enjoyable."

"I'm glad it's your job and not mine. I couldn't handle it."

"I think we're all uniquely suited to follow a certain path. Experience and education plays a part, but most of it is natural talent. That goes for teachers, craftsmen, athletes, and everyone else as much as it does artists and those with psychic abilities."

"I think you're probably right."

Skye yawned. Thad and I looked at him.

"Sorry, it's all the boring conversation." Skye grinned.

"Shut up and eat," I said. Colin laughed.

The four of us had a nice lunch and then we said goodbye. Skye and Thad hugged outside of the Black Heifer. Despite their verbal jousting, I knew that Thad was one of the few guys that Skye truly cared about and the feeling was mutual.

The drive back to Verona was quiet, mostly because Skye and Colin fell asleep. Our trip had been fruitful. I was absolutely certain there was a supernatural explanation for the string of murders. No human could have possibly pulled them off, not even Houdini.

Now it was time to hit the books. I used the Internet extensively for research, but the sources found there were not always trustworthy. My library of books was another matter. I had assembled one of the largest collections on the supernatural in existence. Perhaps the answer lie there.

Chapter Four

I holed up in my library for the next few days. I narrowed down my list of possible suspects, but did not accomplish a good deal more. I was certain the unusual leather was the key, but I had no books on that topic. I wondered if the Verona Historical Society Museum would have any information to offer.

I drove the few blocks to the small museum, located in an old commercial building on a side street downtown. When I arrived the sheriff's car was parked out front with its lights flashing. An ambulance sat nearby. Two EMTs walked toward it. By the time I got out of the hearse and crossed the street the ambulance departed without flashing lights or a siren.

When I neared the entrance, a deputy stopped me. I showed him my ID.

"You're with the FBI? Is that a real ID, Marshall?

I grinned. I had gone to high school with the deputy. Everyone knew everyone else in Verona.

"It's real. If you want to check it out call this number," I said, handing him the card of Agent Heck. "I'm investigating a case. What happened here?"

"A volunteer who was running the museum was found dead when the director returned from lunch. He was murdered."

"How?"

"It looks like he was strangled."

I hurried inside. Mr. Clark, the coroner was hovering over the body. The sheriff stepped toward me. I handed him my ID. He looked at it, then at me skeptically. Before he could speak, his deputy called out.

"His ID is legit."

"You didn't trust me?" I asked, pretending to be surprised.

"Just doing my job."

I retrieved my ID and kneeled down near the body. I couldn't recall the victim's name, but I had often seen him around town. I remembered him as a kindly old man. Now, he was dead. I had to figure this case out before anyone else died. Perhaps this murder had no connection to my case, but the method used to the kill the victim certainly matched.

"Did you find the murder weapon?" I asked.

"No."

"Was the museum open when this happened?"

"Yes."

The murderer could have been anyone then, but I had a feeling our supernatural killer was to blame.

"What do you think was used to kill him?" I asked Dr. Clark.

"Definitely a rope. Look at the bruises and marks on the neck."

There was no question. I could even make out the imprint of a woven rope.

"Whoever killed him used a lot of force, look at the bruising," Dr. Clark said.

"Any ideas on specifics?" I asked. I didn't want to lead him, but I wanted to see if his conclusion matched mine.

"I'd say either a noose or a garrote, probably the later."

Dr. Clark raised the torso and showed me the back of the neck.

"See the space here where there are no marks or bruises? Notice how small it is. The rope was wrapped around the victim's neck and tightened. The more I look at it, the more I believe the killer used a garrote. Even a small noose would leave a larger unblemished area."

I was almost certainly looking at the work of my killer. The marks were nearly identical to the crime scene photos from other cases.

I stood and gazed around the room. Nothing seemed out of place, other than the corpse on the floor.

"Is anything missing?" I asked the museum director.

"No." He paused and walked over to a case not far from the body. "Yes, but..."

I joined him.

"There is something missing, but... it shouldn't be missing. I don't see how it can be."

He walked around the case, examining it, and checked the glass door, which did not budge. Inside the case was a display of early physician artifacts, including an antique doctor's bag, a primitive stethoscope, hand-blown medicine bottles, and other items. There was also an empty space with an untidy pile of antique scalpels and other surgical instruments lying just below it.

"I have the only key to this display case and it's right here," the director said, locating it on his key ring to confirm. "I don't see how anyone got into the case without the key. It's still locked."

I examined the case myself. It was almost entirely made of glass and was intact.

"What's missing?"

"The leather case that held those surgical instruments," he said pointing.

"Can you describe it?"

"It was about 7" by 12" with individual slots for each instrument. Printed on the outside in small letters was 'Dr. Malcolm Mackenzie, Verona, Indiana."

"Did it have any special value?"

"With the original surgical instruments it might have been worth $200 or so, but whoever took it left the instruments. There are far more valuable things in the museum."

"Can you describe the leather?"

"It was odd, very light in color and with an unusual grain."

"Like buckskin?"

"No. This is buckskin," the director said, walking to another case where a Potawatomi pipe bag was on display. "It didn't look anything like buckskin, although the color wasn't far off."

"Do you have any idea what kind of hide it was made from?"

"No, not really. I've never given it much thought. The significance of the piece was that it was a complete scalpel toolkit used by a well-known local doctor."

"Do you have information on this doctor?"

"Certainly. The local historical society published a short biography of him in the 1960s."

"Do you have a copy I can borrow?"

"Here," the director said, walking to a display of historical publications. "You can keep this copy."

"Thank you."

In the time we had talked, the police had finished photographing the crime scene and the body had been placed in a body bag and then on a gurney. I took photos of the surgical instruments that had been in the case while the director talked to the sheriff. I made a few notes and then closed my notebook.

"Thank you for your assistance," I said to the director and then departed. My case had taken an interesting turn.

A few minutes later I sat in front of a crackling fire in a comfortable chair in my room. Halloween was near and the lately warm temperatures had taken on a chill. I sipped hot Yorkshire tea as I read the small booklet about Dr. Malcolm Mackenzie. I skimmed over the early history about the family coming to America in the early 18th century and quickly moved on to the doctor himself. It was unclear when he arrived in Verona, but in 1870 he was practicing medicine here and had a doctor/dentist/undertaker business, which was not as usual for the time as it might seem. Dr. Mackenzie made house calls using his horse and buggy. He performed surgeries, often made his own medicines, and performed autopsies as the county coroner. He was apparently quite successful with curing his patients because patients traveled to Verona from surrounding towns to see him. Travel in late 19th century Indiana was difficult and a journey that took an hour now could take several hours back then so patients coming from fifteen and twenty miles away was a big deal. The doctor remained in Verona until his death in 1916.

There was a great deal of information about the doctor, but I wasn't sure if any of it was of use. I wondered about the last name of Mackenzie. Was he one of Skye's ancestors or was it coincidence?

I carried my mug of tea to the window. A cold rain had started outside and it was darker than it should have been at this hour. It was a good day for ghost stories...or a murder. That thought had occurred to me on similar days before, but it was especially apt now.

I felt a sense of urgency I could not dismiss, but I had little to go on. The supernatural was obviously at work here, but how could I possibly track down the killer with so few clues? It was possible a human could have carried out the last murder, but it was highly unlikely considering the unexplained theft from a locked case and the similarity to the other murders. The method and the missing leather items were the only real connections or clues and what good was that?

My cell phone rang. I pulled it from my pocket and answered.

"It's human skin."

"What?"

"The leather. I finally remembered. It's human skin tanned into leather," Thad said.

"Eww."

Thad laughed, which was rare for Thad. "Does that mean you don't want a wallet made from human skin for Christmas?"

"Yeah, I think I'll pass. Why would anyone tan human skin?" I asked.

"You don't know with your vast knowledge of the supernatural and the macabre?"

"I haven't run into this one before. I vaguely remember something about certain tribes tanning a tattooed section of skin from the deceased, but I don't think that's relevant here."

"I'm sure you'll come up with an answer."

"I hope so. Thank you so much Thad."

"Wait and see if the information is relevant before you thank me."

"Every bit helps."

We talked briefly, then I disconnected.

Human skin. If nothing else, the murders just became a good deal more interesting. I walked to my laptop and began my research.

I looked up when I heard a knock on the door. I glanced at the clock. It was 6 p.m. I had no idea so much time had passed. I crossed the room and opened the door. Skye stood outside.

"Are you going down to supper?"

"Um, yeah."

I stepped out into the hall and walked toward the stairway with Skye.

"You seem distracted."

"I've been doing research for the last few hours. Thad called with some interesting information. He identified the leather. It's human skin."

"Eww."

I laughed. "That was my reaction."

"Why would anyone... never mind. What have you discovered?"

"I've discovered that it's not as rare as you'd think. I found several instances of human skin being used to make leather for various objects. One of the best known is a book in the collection of the Boston Athenaeum library, titled, *Hic Liber Waltonis Cute Compactus Est*. The skin used was that of a notorious nineteenth century highwayman, George Walton, who died of tuberculosis while imprisoned in 1837. Before he died, he requested that his skin be removed and used to bind a volume of his autobiography and be presented to John Fenno, a former robbery victim who had bravely stood up to him after being shot."

"That's a true story? It's not merely online nonsense?"

"I checked it out. The story is true and the book is in the Boston Athenaeum library. It's actually possible to purchase items today made with human skin."

"Is that legal?"

"Yes. A corpse is considered property. While you are alive, your body is yours, but after death you become an object. Hmm, maybe you should bequeath me your body. I could have you stuffed and put on display Skye."

"Very funny."

"It is illegal to sell viable organs that could be used for transplant, but it's perfectly legal to sell body parts otherwise."

"Does this mean you'll be starting a new collection?"

"Um no. I also discovered that while some of the skin used for making leather comes from donors, most often the source is a criminal. Apparently, in the 19th century especially, people wanted souvenirs of notorious murders and highwaymen."

"That could be significant."

"Most certainly. You've heard of Burke & Hare, the Scottish grave robbers?"

"Yes."

"After Burke was hanged, his body was dissected. His skeleton was put on display and several items, including a calling card case, were made from his tanned skin. Sound familiar?"

Skye nodded.

"I think that all the items linked to the murders were made from the skin of a killer."

"Who has come back to seek his revenge?"

"Perhaps or maybe his spirit is out to retrieve his own body parts. Whatever the reason, we just got much closer to solving this string of murders."

"That's great, Marshall, but you could have waited until after supper to tell me all this."

"Think of it as a sort of diet."

"The too grossed out to eat diet?" Skye suggested.

"Think I can market it?"

"Uh, no."

We reached the ground floor and headed for the dining room. There were some two dozen guests already eating, but there was still room for several more at the enormous table. Graymoor Mansion worked very well as a bed & breakfast, but I found it hard to imagine a single family living here. The home was far too vast for one family. Even with dozens of guests it was possible to roam the hallways for extended periods of time without running into another living soul. The dead were another matter, but I alone could see them.

Two large marble-top sideboards were filled with covered dishes. Many of them were heated so one never had to be concerned about cold food. Tonight, there were salads, tomato soup, potato soup, crab cakes, vegetarian lasagna, fettuccini alfredo, and other selections. There were herbed mashed potatoes, asparagus, baby carrots, and more. There were always enough selections to keep everyone happy. There were also a variety of desserts on the sideboard across the room. From a distance I could see a sumptuous looking chocolate cake and a small mountain of petit fours among the other desserts. When I headed in that direction later, I knew I would have difficulty deciding.

I put human leather and supernatural murders out of my mind for a few minutes while I enjoyed eating with Skye and a few of the guests. Colin was not present, but then he often ate at a different time. He was a very busy young man with school, wrestling, workouts, and training with Skye. He shared a suite with Skye so I'm sure he saw his uncle frequently.

I was not a vegetarian, but I selected Caesar salad, vegetarian lasagna, and mashed potatoes along with one of Martha's freshly baked yeast rolls. The food was reason enough to live in Graymoor Mansion, but the atmosphere was incredible, both the beauty of the restored mansion and the supernatural elements. Where else could I live with the mischievous, but often helpful, ghost of a 14th century boy? True, I saw the dead everywhere I went, but Graymoor was one of the most haunted spots in the country. The house had quite a history and attracted ghosts who had nothing to do with the mansion.

I had very nearly moved out on my own a few years ago, but then decided against it. I rented a room and partially paid for it by running ghost tours of the mansion.

I spotted Etienne, the 14th century boy ghost I mentioned earlier, moving about the room watching the guests. Skye barely flinched when Etienne stroked his hair and whispered in his ear. Etienne was particularly fond of Skye and Colin. They were accustomed to him so he did not alarm them. Etienne was fond of handsome boys and young men and often pinched their butts. He did it so frequently he was mentioned in the pamphlet that advertised the b&b and on the website. He also pinched Agent Freeman's butt but that was because he was upset that Freeman didn't believe in ghosts.

I think I could happily remain in the mansion forever exploring its secrets, but I couldn't resist getting out in the world and exploring supernatural mysteries. That's why I set up my business as a supernatural investigator. Many no doubt believed I was a crackpot. Skye had thought so during our high school years until he learned all my 'craziness' was true. There is nothing like experiencing the supernatural to make one a believer.

Over the years I had investigated many hauntings. Most were easy enough for me to solve, especially since I could see and often communicate with the dead, although the latter was much harder than the former. There were others, like the one I was currently investigating, that were much more challenging. Not one of the victims had remained behind, despite their violent deaths so I had to go about things the hard way. Chances were that if I kept investigating crime scenes I would eventually find a victim that haunted the location of his death, but I could not afford to wait. People were dying.

So much for not thinking about the case during supper.

"So how is the gymnasium?" I asked Skye to distract myself.

"It's back in shape. I hate leaving it even for a few days. I don't trust anyone else to maintain the machines."

"I thought about going for a swim later, but with this new information I don't think I'll be able to tear myself away from my computer or the books."

Skye shook his head.

"You can always take a break."

"I'll try, but I doubt it will happen."

"There were some pretty girls in the Natatorium today. They said they would be back."

"Yeah, but they'll only be looking at you."

Skye laughed. "I'll try to tone down my sexiness."

"Yeah, like that's possible."

"Thank you Marshall."

"Grr. I hate it when a compliment slips out!"

"There is nothing wrong with the way you look Marshall."

"That may be so, but when I'm standing beside you I am pathetic in comparison, especially if you aren't wearing a shirt."

"If you come to swim, I'll keep my shirt on and try to stay in the gymnasium. You'll be safe then, unless Colin comes in."

"Grr. Don't remind me that a sixteen-year-old is ten times hotter than me."

"He's my nephew. He can't help it." Skye grinned.

"I'm going to sic Etienne on you."

I looked around, but the boy ghost had moved on to other parts of the mansion. He was often not around when I needed him.

I saved room for dessert. I couldn't decide between chocolate cake and key lime pie, so I had both along with hot tea. Skye limited himself to three petit fours. It was no wonder he had great abs. I suppose I could have too, but it was too much work. The dead did not care how I looked.

I returned to my room and spent the next couple of hours trying to dig up more information on Dr. Mackenzie online. I found a few mentions of him, but nothing I hadn't already read in the publication from the historical society.

When my vision blurred I decided to take a break, perhaps for the night. I grabbed my swimsuit and headed downstairs to the Natatorium. Another advantage of living in Graymoor was access to such amenities as the indoor botanical garden, the library, and the pool.

It was quite a trek to the Natatorium, but the stroll helped my mind to clear. I felt like I should still be at my computer, but I knew my efficiency was impaired and I might miss something important. Often, it was best to step away and come back fresh another day.

I caught the scent of chlorine before I reached the Natatorium, then stepped into the enormous room made almost entirely of glass. The pool was Olympic size, which was impressive considering it was built in the 19th century, a time when it was practically unheard of for a private residence to have an indoor pool.

Around the pool were numerous plants, including some fairly large trees. There were several statues of nude young men, as well as pillars and urns that gave the Natatorium the feel of ancient Greece. Cast iron Victorian pool furniture was interspaced around the pool. The statues, pillars, and furniture were all original to the house, but had been restored to their former glory. A welcome modern addition was the comfy chair and lounge cushions.

A few swimmers were in the pool, but I crossed the space and walked into the locker room without paying much attention. The locker rooms were modern. The men's locker room reminded me of the one at my old high school, except it was a lot nicer and cleaner. Skye kept everything in tiptop shape.

I changed into my swimsuit and put my clothes in a locker. I checked myself out in one of the large mirrors. I looked okay, but I was nothing special. I knew I should put in more time working out, but I wasn't into exercise like Skye.

I spotted Skye when I walked out of the locker room. He was wearing a polo shirt and dressed in shorts, but he still looked gorgeous. He smiled at me apologetically and nodded toward Colin who was shirtless, wet, and dressed in only a skimpy swimsuit. Two high school girls were checking him out as well as a couple of women old enough to be his mother. A few guys were looking him over too. I would never know what it felt like to be the recipient of that kind of attention.

I shrugged, smiled, and jumped into the pool.

It was a wonder that Colin was not conceited. Like his uncle, he pretended to be sometimes and he was aware of his good looks, but he was not stuck on himself.

I was very impressed with Colin because he did not shun those who were not as fortunate as him. He was kind to everyone. Skye said he often asked some of most unattractive girls in his class to dance at school dances. I wondered if he knew how special he made them feel.

No girl would have thought herself special if I asked her to dance in high school. I was considered a freak and even dressed all in black back then until a female friend forced me into a makeover. I was much happier now than I was then. High school could be brutal.

I began to swim. I was here to get some exercise and give my mind a break. Cold rain smacked against the glass roof and walls, but that only made the warmth of the Natatorium and the water more enjoyable. I loved swimming at all times of the year, but it was especially nice now. I also loved to swim in the winter when I could enjoy the warmth and look outside and see falling snow.

My mind relaxed as I swam. I enjoyed the company of the others in the pool even though I was not interacting with them directly. When I grew tired I stood neck high in the swallow end and luxuriated in the feel of the warm water. I amused myself by watching others steal glances of Colin. I wondered what fantasies were going through the minds of the older women.

I pulled myself out of the pool, dried off, then walked into the locker room and changed. I decided not to return to my work. Instead, I'd watch some TV and then sleep. Perhaps tomorrow I would find what I was seeking.

Chapter Five

After breakfast the next morning I closed myself in my room and concentrated on my research. The Internet was filled with false leads, redundant information, and links to genealogical sites. If I wanted to research Dr. Mackenzie's family tree I could have done so, but I needed to discover the link between him and the surgical kit case. The worst part was that I might be completely wasting my time. The doctor might have had no special connection to the case at all. Perhaps the surgical instrument case was a gift and he had no idea it was made from human skin, but if a gift who gave it to him and why? Every possibility created new questions I could not answer.

At lunchtime, I closed my laptop in disgust. I needed a break so I headed downstairs for lunch.

The scents that greeted me as I entered the dining room improved my mood, but did not dispel the overall sense of futility that had descended upon me. I walked to the buffet and selected a steak burrito with Spanish rice and refried beans. I put plenty of sour cream on the burrito. I loved when the mansion served Mexican. It was as good or better than the food found in the best Mexican restaurants.

I sat down across from Sean.

"I'd say 'hi' but you look like you might bite my head off," he said.

"It's been a frustrating morning. I hate the Internet."

I tasted my burrito. "This might just make up for it," I said, pointing to my plate.

Sean smiled. "Maybe you just need to relax, Marshall. You'll get to the bottom of this. You always do."

"The question is, how many people will die before I do? I'm not accustomed to this kind of pressure. Usually no one's life is at stake. At worst, a family can't live in their own home for a while, but this time people are dying."

"That is not your fault and I doubt anyone else could do better. Hell, Marshall, the FBI came to you. I doubt they come to... how shall we say... unconventional investigators very often."

"I know, but that doesn't lessen the sense of urgency. I feel like I'm disarming a ticking time bomb."

"So you haven't found anything useful on this doctor you told me about?"

"No. I can't figure out why he had a surgical kit case made of... you know what," I said. There were other diners near and I did not want to ruin their lunch.

"He was a doctor. My doctor has a real human skeleton in his office. It was used for research at a medical hospital. I'm sure some doctors have other parts."

"It does make more sense than if he was a teacher or lawyer or whatever."

"See."

"Dr. Mackenzie was also the coroner, so he did have access to the raw materials," I said quietly, trying not to be too specific in case anyone overheard.

"Yeah, but I don't think most families would approve of... parts being removed before burial," Sean said.

"True, although there were donors back then, just as we have organ donors now and back in the 19th century some doctors paid grave robbers for cadavers, although that was mostly for medical schools. The kind of leather we're discussing quite often came from executed criminals."

"Maybe you should concentrate on that. Verona has had its share of criminal activity."

"True, but finding a link may be all but impossible."

"All but. You'll succeed, although I must say your dinner conversation leaves much to be desired."

I grinned. "Sorry. It's hard to get my mind off this."

"Let's talk about something else."

"Hmm, I swam in the pool last night. Colin was there. Half the guests were drooling over him."

Sean laughed.

"He was wearing a skimpy little swim-suit. I felt totally inferior."

"Well, he is Skye's nephew. I think a lot of it is in the genes. It shouldn't bother you. We've known Skye for years. Being near him can make anyone feel physically inferior."

"I think I want to be a Mackenzie in my next life."

"Colin's last name isn't Mackenzie."

"You know what I mean."

"Yeah and I'll do you a favor and not tell Skye."

"Not tell Skye what?"

We looked up as Skye neared with a plate of food.

"That you only scored a 50 on your IQ test in high school. We've hidden the truth from you all these years," Sean said.

"Yeah, right. That would make me severely challenged."

"That's why we didn't want to break the news to you," I said.

"Ha! I think you meant my IQ is 150. I feel like a genius."

"Sure you do Skye," I said, patting his shoulder. "Damn, your shoulder is hard as a rock."

"Oh, I see. You were talking about how gorgeous I am and didn't want me to know."

"Wrong again. We were mainly talking about Colin, or I was. That boy makes me feel physically inferior."

Skye laughed.

"I mean it. He's sixteen and compared to him I'm a slug."

"Are you hot for my nephew, Marshall? If so, we have to have a talk. You are too old for him."

"No! You know I'm not into guys and if I was I would not hook up with a high school boy."

"Yeah, I've crossed those off my list too, except for the occasional senior," Skye said.

"Is that friend of Colin's still coming on to you?" Sean asked Skye.

"Uh, yeah. It's annoying, but that's the price of being me."

"Oh lord," I said.

Skye smirked. The three of us talked and laughed through the remainder of lunch. It was exactly the break I needed.

After a piece of banana cream pie, I headed back to my room. I left my laptop closed and turned instead to my own reference library. I searched through the shelves, looking for anything I could find on serial killers and notorious criminals. My hopes were not high because most of my volumes concerned ghosts, supernatural creatures, and magic.

I had hundreds of volumes, so it took a great deal of time just to read the titles on the spines. I was nearly through the whole lot when I spotted it, a tome entitled *Not Jack the Ripper: Little Known Serial Killers of the Nineteenth Century.*

I sat by the fire and paged through the thick tome. I recognized none of the names, which made sense. There were actually very few well-known serial killers from the past. There was Jack the Ripper, of course, and Lizzie Borden, although she was quite likely not guilty of the murders of her parents and two murders does not make one a serial killer. More recent times had more serial killers to offer, but I doubt most could name more than one or two.

More than two-thirds of the way through the book a name caught my eye. Edward Thornton. I had seen the name before, although I could not remember where or when.

My interest increased as I read "responsible for a string of thirteen murders in northern Indiana before he was apprehended." Now we were getting somewhere.

Instead of reading further, I put the book down and closed my eyes. I let my mind search out the name, much as I let it seek out the spirits of the dead when I tried to locate one in a distant location. In my mind, I saw the pages of books, plaques in the historical society, and names on small brass labels on paintings. My mind was drawn toward the edge of town to the cemetery. There it picked up speed and zoomed in on a headstone. My eyes popped open. I knew where I had seen the name before. Edward Thornton was buried in the Verona Cemetery.

I picked up the book and continued to read.

Edward Thornton was a respected citizen and hat maker and maintained a small shop on Main Street in Verona...

There it was in black and white. It was no coincidence. The Edward Thornton buried in the town cemetery was undoubtedly the 19th century serial killer.

Citizens began to notice Thornton acting peculiar several months before the first murder and his strange behavior grew more pronounced as time passed. This behavior was not violent, but was at times frightening, especially when Thornton began jumping out from alleys and shouting at passersby, especially women. Customers began to avoid his previously successful shop and Thornton's financial condition rapidly deteriorated. As his financial worries increased, Thornton's behavior became increasingly troublesome.

Thornton was a suspect after the first murder, but there was no proof of his guilt. An elderly lady, Emma Pinkston, was found strangled to death in her home on the edge of town. Nothing was taken from the home and no motive could be established.

Other murders followed and each victim was strangled with a rope, but no murder weapon could be located. Thornton was caught in the act killing his thirteenth and final victim, Thomas Jenner, a local businessman. The murder weapon was a garrote.

There was little doubt in my mind. The spirit of Edward Thornton had returned.

Thornton was found not guilty by reason of insanity and sent to the Marshall County Insane Asylum, where he died of natural causes in 1872.

A knock at my door pulled me away from the book. I answered to find Skye.

"You're not here to guilt me into a workout are you?"

"Well, it wouldn't hurt you, but I'm actually here to see if you've made any progress on the case."

"Perfect timing. I have."

I motioned Skye inside and we took seats by the fire.

"The killer is Edward Thornton or rather his ghost. He was a 19th century Hoosier serial killer who operated right here in Verona. He was declared not-guilty by reason of insanity."

"So, you're dealing with a crazy ghost?"

"Most certainly. He was a hat maker."

"Is that supposed to tell me something?"

"Surely you have heard the phrase 'mad as a hatter'?"

"Yeah. Isn't that from *Alice in Wonderland*?"

"No. It's earlier, but there is a reason for the Mad Hatter in *Alice in Wonderland*. In the 19th century hat makers used mercury in the hat making process. A good many of them came down with mercury poisoning and one of the symptoms is madness. No one knew what was causing so many hat makers to go insane, but that is where the phrase 'mad as a hatter' originated."

"So what is the connection between the leather items and this mad hatter?"

"Human leather often comes from convicted criminals. Thornton was found innocent because of his insanity, but there was no doubt he killed thirteen people. It's my guess that someone was given custody of his body after death and I'm almost certain that someone was Dr. Mackenzie. He possessed a surgical instrument case made of human leather and he was the doctor and coroner in Verona when Thornton died. I believe he autopsied or studied the body and then used the skin to make leather, which he had made into various objects as souvenirs."

"Who would want something like that?"

"Souvenirs of killers were big during the Victorian age."

"Couldn't they have collected stamps instead?"

"People in the Victorian era did some odd things, such as make wreaths out of human hair and take photos of dead people."

"What?" Skye asked.

"It seems bizarre and even macabre to us, but it had to do with remembrance. A hair wreath might be made from the hair of the entire family or just an individual. They were usually put in frames behind glass. It was a way of remembering family members. It was the same with post mortem photos. We can snap digital photos to our heart's content now, but back then photography was expensive, so expensive most couldn't afford it. If someone died young, the only way to have a photo was to take one after they died."

"I think I'd just as soon not have a photo at all."

"There were likely those who thought that way then too. The point is that the Victorians weren't as squeamish about such things as we are now."

"Okay, but when Christmas comes around I don't want any gifts made from body parts."

"Well, there goes that idea."

"So what next?"

"I'll see if I can confirm my theory. I'm off to the historical society in the morning."

"You live a life of excitement Marshall."

"Grr."

Skye departed soon after. Research could yield its own excitement. In this case it might even help save lives.

The next morning after a breakfast of eggs benedict, French toast, bacon, and hot tea I drove to the historical society and asked if they had any records of Dr. Mackenzie. I was directed to a computer where digital copies of documents, newspapers, and other paper items were stored. A search for 'Malcolm Mackenzie' brought up a surprising number of hits including newspaper articles and some of his medical records. I realized I could be here for days if I didn't narrow my search parameters further so I searched for 'Malcolm Mackenzie' and 'Edward Thornton." The number of results dropped to one.

I brought up Dr. Mackenzie's medical records and at least part of my theory was immediately proven. The doctor had not only performed an autopsy on Edward Thornton, but a dissection. He even removed Thornton's brain and studied it for abnormalities that could have been the cause of his madness. The preserved brain was sent to Indiana University for further study.

Soon, I found conformation for the rest of my theory. The doctor's records spoke of removing the epidermal layer and taking it to the local tanner. At the bottom was even a description of the leather, noting the light coloration and odd texture when compared to other leather. I was right. Dr. Mackenzie had skinned the hatter and presumably had the leather made into a case for his surgical instruments and other items that he likely gave away as souvenirs of the serial killer. Now, Thornton was back to retrieve his skin and he killed anyone who possessed one of the items made from his skin or were in close proximity to those items.

I wondered why Thornton had waited so long to claim his skin and take his revenge. Perhaps he was at rest until recently. Some spirits lay dormant until something disturbed them. Perhaps he had been at his task for decades, but had accelerated his efforts. The reason did not matter. All that mattered now is that the body count was climbing.

I returned to Graymoor Mansion and my own computer. I began a search for items made of human leather that might have a connection to the Mad Hatter. If I could find the items, I could figure out where he would strike next.

Four hours later I had found nothing. I had turned up plenty of information on artifacts made from human leather and even a few museums that had such artifacts on display, but I couldn't

91

pin any of them down to the source. It was time to call in some help.

***

"So, I'm waiting to hear from Agent Heck. I hope the FBI can turn up something. I came up with a big zero," I said as I finished bringing Skye, Colin, and Sean up to speed on my progress as we ate in a small private dining room in the mansion.

"Well, they do have better resources than the Internet," Sean said.

"True. If they can't come up with anything, I think my next step is to contact every museum with a piece on display and see if they can tell me about the origins of their artifacts, but that will take a great deal of time. What worries me is the pieces in private hands. These pieces have been floating around for more than a century. There is no way of knowing how many pieces were made from Thornton's remains or where they are now."

"And owning any of them is like possessing a time bomb and not knowing it," Skye said.

"Exactly. That's why we have to stop the Mad Hatter," I said taking a sip of my tea. We were up to dessert now. The warm peach cobbler was delicious.

"How do you stop a ghost?" Skye asked.

"On *Supernatural* they burn the remains," Colin said.

"I think we need to stick to reality," Skye said.

"Actually, that would force his spirit into the next world, but unfortunately Thornton's remains are likely spread out all over the country, perhaps even the world. Finding all the pieces would be virtually impossible."

"So, how will you stop him?" Sean asked.

"Often, I can convince a spirit to move on, but since this one is insane that isn't an option."

"Ghosts can be insane?" Colin asked.

"Spirits keep the personality they had when living for the most part. They change once they move on, but usually not before.

"I'll need to exorcise him. Since he's insane, I'll have to trap him first."

"How?" Colin asked.

"The easiest way is with a ring of salt.   We'll lure him in, close the ring and he will be trapped."

"That's on *Supernatural* too!" Colin said.

I glared.

"Sorry, but it is."

"I know.   Where do you think the producers got the information?"

Colin's eyes widened. "You mean you..."

"We'll talk about it later."

"How do you plan to lure him in?" Skye asked.

"That's where you come in."

"Why don't I like the sound of that?"

"Well... we need a victim."

"Gee. Thanks."

"I'll do it!" Colin said.

"No you won't," Skye and I said together.

"Sure, gang up on me."

"It's going to be dangerous, but you have the best chance of any of us of coming out of this alive.   If we don't do something, more people will die."

"I'm in," Skye said without hesitation.

My cell rang.   I stepped away from the table as the others talked and ate their desserts.   In less than five minutes, I was back.

"There are two institutions that have artifacts that can be traced to Dr. Mackenzie and the Mad Hatter.   One is a county museum in Pennsylvania.   The other is the Children's Museum in Indianapolis."

"The Children's Museum? Oh my god," Sean said.

"Don't worry.   On my recommendation the museums are being closed and cleared.   Within an hour there will be no one inside either of them.   Pack your bag, Skye, we're going to Indianapolis.   I want to leave as soon as possible."

In half an hour we were on our way.   Indianapolis was only about two hours or so from Verona so it was not a long journey.

We drove straight to the museum. There were three state police cars parked outside as well as a black sedan.

We stepped out. Night had come, but light shined from inside the museum. I had never visited, but it was an impressive multi-story structure that, at least from the front, was mostly constructed of glass.

"I'm sorry, but the museum is closed..." one of the state troopers begin. Skye and I showed him our IDs. "Right this way," he said, leading us to two familiar men in suits.

"Agent Heck. Agent Freeman," I said nodding.

"The building has been cleared and locked. The chair, table, and supplies you requested are set up and the artifact has been brought out of storage. It's on the table as you instructed."

"Good. I have no idea how long this will take, but no one comes in. Period."

"We'll leave it to you. I admit I don't mind staying outside," Agent Heck said.

"Let's do it," I said.

Agent Blake led us to the front entrance, unlocked it, and then relocked it after we were inside.

"I guess you feel really important right now," Skye said with a smirk.

"Shut up or I'll take my time exorcising him."

I didn't waste any time, not even to examine the artifact. I picked up the two boxes of salt and began to make a circle around the table, leaving an area directly behind the chair open. Once that was done I peered at the artifact. It was a belt with a hand-forged buckle. It didn't look all that different from any other belt except for the light color. No one would have guessed it was deadly.

"Are you ready?" I asked.

"I was born ready."

"So take a seat and prepare to be a victim."

"You know if this goes wrong and he strangles me I am coming back to haunt you," Skye warned.

"Why do you think I'm going to make sure it doesn't go wrong? A little of you goes a long way. I can't imagine being stuck with you forever."

I moved into the shadows. Skye said alone at the table. Few would be brave enough to do what he was doing, but Skye possessed extraordinary bravery. He knew he was taking a great risk. If this went wrong... No. I would not let that happen and Skye was far from powerless.

The minutes crept by and slowly turned into hours. I hated waiting. It was one of my least favorite things, but it my profession there was sometimes a great deal of it. Skye appeared to be at least partially dozing off, but I could not allow myself to do so. No matter what happened I had to remain alert.

I popped a caffeine pill, swallowing it without water. I was thirsty, but a bathroom break was not an option so neither Skye nor I had drunk anything since the moment we set out for Indy. The first thing I was going to do when this was over was find the nearest water fountain.

Time passed slowly with absolutely nothing happening. Then, I could suddenly see Skye's breath. That meant the air around him was growing colder which was a sign that a spirit was near. I saw Skye tense slightly. He knew this was it.

I peered intently at Skye and the area directly behind him but could see nothing. Then, as if a switch had been flipped he appeared, dressed in a tattered suit and top hat—The Mad Hatter. The garrote appeared around Skye's neck, just as the Mad Hatter himself had appeared. No wonder the Hatter's victims had no chance.

Even as I moved forward Skye attempted to stand, but abruptly sat again. I knew why. Standing only tightened the garrote around his neck. He wisely fell to the side even as I rushed forward, closed the ring of salt, and began to chant.

The Mad Hatter must have realized what was happening for even as he tightened the garrote to finish the task he stiffened and turned toward me, losing his grip in the process. Skye took advantage of the Hatter's lapse and dove over the circle of salt. The garrote was still around his neck, but with no one to tighten it was not a threat to his life.

The Mad Hatter circled, looking for an escape, but there was none for him now. He threw himself against the invisible barrier even as I chanted louder. He made the effort again and again, but it was futile. As I neared the end of the exorcism, he became as solid as a living being for a few moments. I could tell he was visible even to Skye, who looked on the spirit's shocked, anguished, crazed, and terrified expression with pity. The Hatter continued to fight to leave the circle, but every time he hit the barrier he rebounded as if he'd hit a solid wall. I completed the exorcism and in an explosive flash of light the Mad Hatter dissolved into a pile of bone and dust.

The air immediately warmed and I smiled.

"He'll be okay now. He won't suffer anymore and no one else will die," I said.

Skye had cut off the garrote while I preformed the exorcism. He rubbed his throat.

"I couldn't see him until the very end."

"His victims could not see him at all. They were doomed."

We walked to the entrance and tapped on the door. One of the officers unlocked it and let us out.

"It's done," I said.

"For a few moments, I thought I saw…" said one of the officers.

"You did."

"What was that flash of light?" asked another.

"That was a spirit moving on to the next world."

I smiled slightly at the officer's confused features. We walked to Agents Heck and Freeman.

"All that remains are dust and bone fragments. When he materialized in the present, his body aged and decomposed 100 years in a matter of seconds. That said, if you do a DNA test on the remains, I believe you'll find it matches the DNA of the tanned artifact in this museum as well as the tanned artifact in the museum in Pennsylvania."

"Okay, I believe in ghosts now. I've never seen anything like that before," Agent Freeman said.

I grinned. "I knew you'd come around. Etienne will be pleased."

***

Skye, Colin, Sean, and I met for supper in a small private dining room on the first floor once again. I had slept most of the day because Skye and I didn't get in until well past dawn. When

I did arise, I took it easy because downtime was rare for me. At any minute, the phone could ring and I'd be off on another case, although most likely not as a special investigator for the FBI

Roasted chicken, mashed potatoes, green beans, baby carrots, cranberry sauce, and freshly baked rolls sat on the table. A chocolate cake sat beside a small stack of plates on a marble-top sideboard at the edge of the room. We all helped ourselves, then sat back in the comfortable chairs and ate while we talked about recent events.

Skye and I regaled Colin and Sean with our exploits in the Children's Museum while a fire crackled away in the hearth. I, for one, was glad to be done with the matter.

"So are you and Marshall going into business together?" Sean asked Skye.

"Hardly. This was a one-time thing for me. I'll leave the supernatural investigations to Marshall. I prefer foes who do not possess otherworldly powers."

"What's wrong Skye? Was it too scary for you?"

"Don't make me hurt you Marshall."

"Don't mess with me or I'll sic Etienne on you."

Skye jumped. I knew Etienne had pinched him. I grinned at Skye as he rubbed his butt.

I wasn't sure what I would investigate next, a simple haunting, a possession, a ghost hound, or even a string of murders, but one thing was for sure; I couldn't wait.

Poste Mortem
The Witch of Wolf Creek

Chapter One
Verona, Indiana
November 2007

A flash of lightning brilliantly illuminated my room in The Graymoor Mansion for a moment and was followed almost instantly by a deafening clap of thunder. As the sound of the thunder diminished I heard an insistent knocking at my door.

"Colin?" I asked as I opened the door to discover Skye's nephew and two dripping wet high school boys standing in the hallway.

"Can we come in? Riley and Tor need your help."

"Of course. Stand by the fire. I'll get towels."

As I walked into the bathroom, I wondered why Colin had brought two soaked and shivering boys to my room at 9 p.m. on a blustery November night, but I had no doubt I would soon learn.

I returned with the towels and handed them to the boys.

"They need dry clothing," I said.

"I'll get some of mine. We're about the same size. Be right back!" Colin said and promptly departed.

"Maybe a hot shower is a better idea. You guys can use my bathroom."

"Thank you," one of them said, his teeth chattering. Both boys walked into my bathroom and disappeared. I pulled out my phone and called the kitchen downstairs.

"Martha? Could you have some hot cocoa sent up to my room? Enough for four? Some cookies would be nice too. I just received some cold and wet visitors."

"I'll send it right up."

"Thanks, Martha."

Martha Merlot was the head chef of The Graymoor Mansion Bed & Breakfast. She had a small staff to help, but she was nearly always to be found in the kitchen.

I crossed to the fireplace and added another log. I wondered what the boys showering in my bathroom had been doing out on this cold rainy night and more importantly, what happened to them. The cold was not the only reason they shivered. I had read terror in their eyes.

"Where are they?" Colin asked when he returned a few minutes later.

"In my bathroom. I suggested a hot shower. I didn't think merely drying off would be enough. They, uh... went into together."

"They're on my wrestling team. They're used to showering with other guys."

"I'm having cocoa and cookies sent up. What happened?"

"I'm not sure, but they were pretty freaked out when they arrived. Tor said ghosts tried to kill them."

My eyebrow raised and my interest increased. Colin disappeared into the bathroom to deliver the clothes and then returned.

The storm outside increased in intensity, sending icy rain hurtling onto the windowpanes. The lightning was so close and frequent that my room was brightly illuminated every few seconds. The thunder was so loud it drowned out the sound of the shower running in the bathroom.

The cocoa and cookies arrived before the boys returned, so I set the trays on the low table between two Victorian armchairs before the fireplace. Colin and I moved a loveseat in closer facing the fire so the four of us could sit and talk.

"Thank you," one of the boys said as he emerged from my bathroom, now wearing Colin's clothing.

"Yeah, thanks. We hung up the towels," said the other.

"You're welcome. Take the chairs by the fire and have some hot cocoa and cookies."

"Marshall, this is Riley and Tor. Guys, this is Marshall, the guy I'm always talking about," Colin said.

Both boys were about Colin's age, sixteen, and muscular, which was no surprise since they were on Colin's wrestling team at Verona High School. Both also had brown hair, but Riley's eyes were brown while Tor's were blue.

We didn't speak immediately. I gave the boys some time to eat and warm up further. Riley jumped slightly as another bolt of lightning filled the room with bright light.

"Colin mentioned that ghosts tried to kill you," I said after eating a cookie and drinking most of a cup of cocoa myself.

"I know. It sounds crazy, but it's true," Tor said.

"It doesn't sound crazy to me. Tell me what happened."

The boys looked at each other for a moment and then Tor began speaking.

"We spent the day exploring and lost track of the time. Evening came on while we were still far outside of town. We had flashlights in our pockets so it wasn't a big deal, but then the storm came in.

"Things didn't get unpleasant until we were a couple of miles from town. We walked through an old section of forest where we'd walked lots of times before, but it was... different and not just because of the storm."

"Different how?" I asked.

"It felt... wrong."

"Sinister," Riley added.

"Then it got weird. There's nothing out there except huge trees, some of them gnarled into weird shapes, and the ruins of an old stone well."

"And we found that tombstone once too," Riley said.

"Yeah, but tonight and this is going to sound really weird, but there was a village there, only it wasn't entirely there."

"What do you mean?" I asked.

"There were like... log cabins and wooden and stone houses. There was a church and a graveyard, but none of it seemed quite... real," Riley said.

"Or solid. It was like a hologram or a projection of a village, but part of it seemed solid in a way most of it was not. It's hard to explain. It was there, but it wasn't," Tor said.

"Interesting," I said.

"We were plenty spooked and yet curious until they, the ghosts that is, came. There were two of them. They weren't there and then suddenly they were."

"Can you describe them?" I asked.

"They were silvery-blue and looked transparent part of time, but more real at other times. One was maybe our age and the other older, like maybe thirty? I don't know. We didn't stick around to gawk," Tor said.

"We ran like hell, especially when they came after us," Riley said.

"What happened then?" I asked, glancing at Colin.

"One of the grabbed me," Riley said. "He hit me. The other one almost got me too, but Tor grabbed my arm and pulled me away, then we ran and didn't stop running until we arrived here."

"It's very unusual for a ghost to attack or to be able to attack," I said.

"I'm not lying. I can prove it."

Riley pulled up his shirt. There were fresh bruises on his side and chest. I did not doubt his word, but if I had, the proof would have erased the doubt.

"I know you're not lying. I'm quite certain you are telling the truth." Colin gazed at me a moment. He knew what I meant.

"It was the scariest thing that's ever happened to me. I'm not ashamed to admit I screamed and maybe even cried a little," Tor said, taking another sip of cocoa.

"I think they would have killed me if Tor hadn't rescued me," Riley said. "The young one got me. The expression on his face was murderous."

"Do you think they're safe now?" Colin asked.

I nodded.

"Whatever attacked them didn't follow them."

"How can you be sure?" Riley asked.

"I can see the dead."

"Like that kid in *The Sixth Sense*?"

"Something like that. Most ghosts tend to remain in a specific place, but not always. You should be safe, although I can't guarantee it."

"Can we wear something like garlic around our necks?" Tor asked.

I smiled.

"No. The only thing that will hold a ghost or keep it out is salt."

"Salt? Why?"

"That's a great question and no one knows the answer, but it's true."

"You're sure?"

"Absolutely. If you put a ring of salt around your bed you can sleep assured no ghost will harm you. The ring must be unbroken for it to work."

"I'm grabbing some salt when I get home," Riley said.

"I'd like to check out the location where this happened," I said.

"I don't want to go back there," Tor said.

"I know where it is. I've been there. We've been there," Colin said, looking at the other boys.

"Good enough then."

"So you believe us?" Tor asked, as if he couldn't believe that I believed.

"Absolutely. I deal with things like this often."

"Colin said you did and, well, we believed him and yet..." Riley said.

"It's almost impossible to believe?" I asked.

"Yeah, except not anymore," Riley said.

"Encountering a ghost is the usual way in which a doubter or unbeliever learns that ghosts truly do exist."

"We've walked through that woods a hundred times and nothing has ever happened before. We've even been there at night. We've camped out there, but tonight..." Tor said.

"Something generally causes a manifestation. You mentioned a tombstone. Perhaps someone disturbed a grave. There are endless reasons that spirits become active. The village is another matter. There have been sightings of ghost homes and even trains, but I've never come across an account of an entire ghost village. I'm intrigued."

"So you'll check it out?" Tor asked.

"Try to stop him from checking it out," Colin said with a grin.

"You should be careful about who you tell about this," I said.

"Because they'll think we're nuts?" Riley asked.

"Yes, but in this case stirring up curiosity about the site could be dangerous. The next person who is attacked might not be so lucky."

"I'm not telling anyone," Tor said.

"Me either. We wouldn't have told you if Colin hadn't told us about you."

"You did come to the right place. Feeling warmer?"

"Yes, thank you. We should get going."

"I can drive you home. You don't want to get soaked all over again, especially not when it's this cold outside. I will warn you, my car is unconventional."

"I've seen it in town," Tor said. Riley nodded.

"So are you guys okay with riding it in? You can ride in the front."

"If we can survive an encounter with ghosts who tried to kill us, we can handle riding in a hearse," Riley said.

"You should try the back. It's comfy!" Colin said.

"Uh, no thanks."

We walked downstairs. I had the boys wait with Colin while I brought the hearse around close to the entrance. Even in my raincoat I got a bit wet and trembled with the chill. I didn't even want to think how Tor and Riley had felt when soaked.

The boys dashed for the car when I stopped. Colin waved from the doorway, then turned and shut the door.

"Oh man, this is freaky," Riley said as I drove toward the gate.

"Don't worry, the back is empty. If there was a ghost there I would see it."

"How can you handle dealing with supernatural stuff? Those ghosts scared the crap out of me," Tor said.

"It's what I do. Ghosts have fascinated me my entire life. I find them more fascinating than frightening."

"Do you ever get scared?"

"Oh yeah. The average ghost doesn't frighten me, but there are things out there that... well, you're better off not knowing."

"This is some storm," Riley said as the windshield wipers worked at high speed. I was driving slower than usual because it was difficult to see.

"Yeah, you didn't pick a good evening to stay out late."

"Tell me about it," Tor said.

I dropped off Riley first, then followed Tor's direction to his house.

"Thanks for everything."

"Thank you for sharing your encounter with me."

Tor opened the door and bolted for his home. Once he was inside I drove back to The Graymoor Mansion.

I stopped by the kitchen when I returned and made myself a mug of hot tea, which I carried up to my room. I settled in by the fire and thought about the tale Tor and Riley had told me. As I told them, I was certain they told me the truth. What I did not tell them is that I had psychic abilities including a limited ability to read thoughts. I never intruded without permission, but I had brushed over the thoughts of Tor and Riley just enough to know that they firmly believed the story they had related.

I had never heard of a village so close to Verona. I wasn't especially well versed in local history, but it seemed to me that I would have heard something about a village that was located only a couple of miles from town, even if it had all but vanished. I did not believe I was familiar with the site myself, but then there was apparently little physical evidence it had ever existed. From the description given by the boys, I would say what they witnessed dated to the mid-nineteenth century. It couldn't be much earlier because few outside of the Native Americans inhabited northern Indiana before that time. I considered searching online for information, but I didn't have enough data to even begin.

The next day was Monday so checking out the site had to wait until Colin had finished his day at school, as well as wrestling practice. I put the time to good use and headed for the local historical museum where I hoped to find the director, George Madison.

The bells rang on the door as I entered. The museum was housed in an old store building on Main Street, not far from Ofarim's. The first floor of the building was mostly filled with glass cases of artifacts from Verona's past, everything from a coverlet woven by Martha Selby in 1848 to a uniform worn by a local boy in WWI. Outside the cases were such items as a butter churn, flax wheel, and an early Maytag washing machine.

"Marshall, what brings you in?"

"The search for information, of course."

"What is it this time?"

"Do you know of a village that once existed near Verona, about two miles from here?"

"Wolf Creek."

"You do know everything, don't you?"

"I can't make that claim, but I am familiar with Verona's past. Your obsession is the supernatural, mine is local history."

"I've never heard of Wolf Creek."

"I'm not surprised. It disappeared sometime around 1844."

"Disappeared?"

"It was abandoned after a series of suspicious deaths and disappearances. The few residents who remained packed up and moved on. I'm not surprised you haven't heard of Wolf Creek. It only existed for about five years and the population probably never exceeded three-dozen, but in that short time a school/church was constructed and Wolf Creek had its own store. A lot of small communities grew and then fizzled out in the early years. Wolf Creek may well have disappeared on its own, but the survivors had reason to move on. For years it was considered a cursed location. There is next to nothing left of it now."

"Interesting. Are there any newspapers from Wolf Creek or written accounts?"

"Wolf Creek never had a newspaper. To date, the only mention I've found about it was in the county history published in 1900 and it doesn't have much to say beyond what I just told you. Of course, there is a lot of material in the archive that hasn't been studied or cataloged yet. Why the sudden interest?"

"Keep this to yourself, but two boys came to me last night and claimed that a ghost village appeared about two miles out of town in a location where they once found a grave marker and where there are the ruins of an old stone well."

"That's Wolf Creek, but a ghost village?"

"I'm convinced they were telling the truth. What's more, they claimed to have been attacked by ghosts and one had bruises to prove it."

George led me back to his office where we sat in comfortable chairs and I told him everything Tor and Riley had told me, withholding only their names.

"You know, Marshall, there was a time I would have dismissed that story as nonsense, but I've lived in Verona too long to dismiss such things out of hand. I've seen things with my own eyes that I wouldn't be comfortable relating to others. There was also that incident here last month. Who would have thought that a seemingly innocent artifact on display would lead to a murder?"

"Experiencing is believing. A great many guests scoff at the idea of ghosts when they arrive at the bed & breakfast, but their attitudes are quite different when they depart."

"Do you think there is real danger again this time?"

"That's what I fear. That's why I'm checking it out."

"Well, I can't help you with ghosts, but I will do everything I can to help with research on Wolf Creek. Let's go back to the archives. I'll show you our cataloged material. I have a couple of volunteers who come in the afternoons who are trying to organize all the materials that have piled up over the years. I'll tell them to keep an eye out for anything pertaining to Wolf Creek."

George led me into the back where floor-to-ceiling shelves holding masses of papers, books, pamphlets, and various artifacts occupied nearly the entire space. Two long tables, one surrounded with chairs took up the only area free of shelving.

"Whoa," I said.

"Yeah. We're in the process of digitizing everything we can, beginning with the most fragile items. Books and documents on rag paper can last for centuries, but some of the more modern stuff yellows and grows brittle quite quickly. Ideally, all this would be organized, indexed, and cataloged, but we have very limited resources and staff."

The bells on the door rang up front.

"I'll leave you to it. Feel free to look at anything you want."

"Thanks, George."

The task was almost too daunting to begin, but I could eliminate a lot of the material stored in the archives. Anything pertaining to Wolf Creek would date to right around the 1840's.

I began with the shelves on the right side of room. I carefully scanned the books, documents, and other materials, stopping to examine any that looked as if they might date to the correct time period. Even so, it was slow going and my chances of success were slim.

I remained in the archives for a few hours. George came back to help when he could. The volunteers joined me after lunch, but when it was time to depart to pick up Colin all I had earned for my efforts was a slight headache.

109

I drove the short distance to VHS, making only a short detour to Ofarim's, and then parked behind the school and waited for Colin to emerge. Evening came on even as I waited for Colin. The days were fast growing shorter and would only continue to do so until the winter solstice.

Colin emerged from the gymnasium several minutes later with some of his teammates.

He naturally had no trouble spotting the hearse and climbed in.

"I'm starving!" Colin said.

I pointed to the cardboard tray in the seat between us.

"That is all for you."

"Oh, I love you Marshall!"

"Everyone does."

"You sound like Skye."

"Hey, is that a nice thing to say about someone who bought you food from Ofarim's? I even brought a milkshake."

"I considered it a compliment, but don't tell Skye that."

"Your secret is safe with me. Which direction?" I asked.

"It's out past the old Chamberlain house."

"How are your friends?" I asked as I pulled out.

"Still a little freaked out, but not bad considering."

"A ghost attack does tend to unsettle most."

"Except for you, of course."

"Yeah, it happens to me all the time."

Colin grinned.

"So what do you hope to find where we're going?" Colin asked between bites of burger.

"Wolf Creek."

"Wolf Creek?"

"That was the name of the village."

"So there really was a village there at one time?"

"Yes, for a few years until about 1844 when it was abandoned."

"An entire village was abandoned, just like that?"

"Well, I doubt it happened overnight, but those who lived there had good reason to leave. The residents of Wolf Creek abandoned it because of a series of unexplained murders and disappearances."

"Uh oh, you've got that gleam in your eye again."

"What gleam?"

"The one Skye warned me about; the gleam you get when you latch onto a mystery and won't let go."

"You guys know me too well."

We drove past the old Chamberlain place, another relic of the 19th century, and then yet farther out of town.

"Pull in to that abandoned drive. This is as close as we can get in a car," Colin said.

We climbed out. I opened the back and retrieved my backpack.

"Thanks for Ofarim's. I'm good for at least an hour now," Colin said.

I shook my head. The boy could eat.

"I don't think I've ever been out this way," I said.

"There isn't a lot out here except woods and farmland. I came exploring with some of the guys."

We walked past the remnants of an old homestead. There was nothing left except for a basement that was slowly filling in and the ruins of an old barn. I didn't detect any spirits here so whoever had once lived here had gone on.

Just past an overgrown meadow we entered a forest. The leaves had already fallen from the trees, except for some oaks which would cling to their dead brown leaves until the next spring. The dry leaves crunched underfoot, sending two deer flying. A squirrel chattered us from above, none too happy we'd disturbed him.

Much sooner than I expected Colin halted.

"There it is."

"This is it? There really isn't much here," I said.

"Come on, I think I can find the well."

I followed Colin through the tall grass. There truly was little to see and no evidence that a village once stood here. The only hint was the openness of the area. There were fewer trees here. I could almost picture a small village in my mind; homes with gardens and pens for livestock, with fields beyond the village. Then again, the lack of trees was no evidence for the existence of Wolf Creek. A forest had plenty of time to grow here since 1844.

"Here it is," Colin said.

Before us was a ring of cut stones about two feet high. It was all that was left of an old well. The opening was covered with old boards and tangled barbed wire. A very faded sign read, "Danger. Unstable well."

Using the well as a center point, I began to walk in a spiral and soon almost tripped over a foundation stone that protruded from the earth by only three or four inches. The foundation was mostly hidden by the grass, but by stepping around in the area I was able to ascertain that a building that measured about fifteen by fifteen once stood here. The foundation was very old and made of hand-cut sandstone.

Colin and I explored the site and uncovered more evidence that structures had once stood here. There was very little to see. What we discovered we found mostly by the feel of hard stone underfoot.

"This is definitely it."

"It wouldn't make much of a historic site, would it?" Colin said.

"Like you're interested in historic sites."

"They aren't all completely boring, just mostly. I'm glad I never lived here. I bet it was boring when it was inhabited."

"Perhaps, at least until the murders and disappearances began."

"Yeah, a murder always livens things up. Any sign of Riley and Tor's ghosts?"

I shook my head.

"This place has an odd feel to it, but it's a resonance of tragedy. I'm not picking up on the presence of any spirits."

"See? This place was so boring even the ghosts didn't stick around."

"It's certainly not very active."

"You're not beginning to doubt Riley and Tor are you?"

"No. They believed the account they gave me and Riley had bruises. They were telling me what they believed to be the truth."

"Does that mean it might not have happened and that they only think it did?"

"It's a possibility. The mind can make one see and experience things that aren't really there."

"Seriously?"

"Certainly. We all see things that aren't there on a daily basis. The mind works in patterns. When it can't identify what the eyes are seeing it manufactures images that best fit."

"You're putting me on."

"No. It's true. The mind also suppresses information that it doesn't deem important so that it can focus on what is. That's why illusionists are able to make things seem to appear and disappear. They take advantage of how the mind works."

"Wow."

"There are also times that the neurons fire without a stimulus.

"What do you mean?"

"If I make a fist and move it toward your face as if I'm going to hit you, the neurons in your brain fire to let you know you're in danger of getting hit in the face. Sometimes, a brain malfunctions and causes one to see the fist coming, when there is no fist."

"Damn."

"There was a case of a patient in a mental hospital that periodically began to scream and attempt to escape from what she claimed was a ball of fire. There was no ball of fire. Those working on her case believe that her neurons fired without a stimulus so she actually saw a ball of fire and felt its heat, even though it wasn't there."

"That's freaky."

"Yes."

"So how can anyone be sure anything is real?"

"You can't."

"Okay, you're blowing my mind now."

"Well, you are blond. It's not that difficult a task."

"Hey!"

"I was only making sure you were listening. I don't believe that what your friends experienced was generated in their minds."

"Then where is the ghost village? Where are the ghosts?"

"The appearance of both could be time dependent. Certain manifestations occur only at a certain time of day or even on a certain date."

"So this could be a once a year thing?"

"Or once every fifty or a hundred years. There is no way of knowing. Perhaps, we only need to wait."

"If we're waiting for night, it almost here," Colin said.

I pulled off my backpack and took out two flashlights. I handed one to Colin.

"If we happen to get separated, go straight back to the car."

"What do you think is going to happen?"

"I don't know, possibly nothing, but it's best to be prepared. Let's keep looking."

As the darkness deepened we stumbled across yet more foundations. We also found a tombstone that could have been the one mentioned by the boys, but the lettering was so weathered all I could make out was the date 1839. I had no idea if it indicated birth or death. In the same vicinity we found other grave markers, all lying flat and nearly all so worn nothing could be made out except for a name or partial date here and there. We discovered nothing of significance to the case, but there was no doubt there was once a village in what looked like nothing more than an overgrown meadow now.

The feel of the site abruptly shifted. As the boys had said, it suddenly felt off or wrong. The wind picked up, stirring dead and then a spectral village began to shimmer into existence around us. First one structure, then another, then more appeared.

"Whoa," Colin said.

I turned in a circle. There were homes made of stone and even more constructed of hand-hewn logs. Most were one-story, but here and there was a two-story structure. Near the edge of the village was what looked like it a church. Near it, a graveyard appeared where we had discovered the ruined markers.

"This is utterly cool."

Most boys would have been terrified in such a situation, but not Colin. He had lived in The Graymoor Mansion for over a year now and was well-accustomed to the supernatural goings-on there. Colin had a ghost cat for a pet and a ghost boy for an admirer.

I shined my flashlight on a structure nearby that had the look of a store. The light did little to illuminate the sign out front, which did not surprise me since the structure both was and was not there. Even so I was able to make out "Dry Goods" and "Photography." The last was peculiar since photography studios were not widespread until later.

I didn't have time to ponder because I became aware of a most malignant presence forming nearby.

"We're leaving. Now!" I said, grabbing Colin's wrist and running in the direction of the car. I thought I heard or felt something pursuing us at first, but if so it quickly gave up. Even so, I did not rest easy until we were in the hearse and driving back toward The Graymoor Mansion.

"What happened?" Colin asked.

"I felt something rather nasty take form near us. I have little doubt it was the murderous ghosts. I'm not ready to confront them and I'd rather not do it with you there."

"You know I can take care of myself."

"Yes, but your Uncle Skye might not approve and I don't want to get on his bad side."

"Afraid of Skye huh?"

"I would be if something happened to you on my watch."

"It will never happen," Colin said. Like uncle, like nephew.

Back at the mansion, I pondered what I had seen as I paced in my room. I was quite excited. I had read accounts of spectral barns, homes, and even trains, but I couldn't remember an account of an entire village and had certainly never witnessed any such thing for myself.

I wondered if the manifestation had only recently started or if it had been going on for some time. The site was just remote enough that it was unlikely that anyone would happen through the area at night.

I wondered even more about the ghosts. I had read nothing in the literature about ghosts appearing along with spectral buildings and certainly not murderous ghosts. I had little doubt that the spirit that I sensed had evil intent. It was that intent I had felt. We didn't stick around long enough for me to see the apparition, but see it I would for I intended to go back when I had learned more.

I turned to the Internet, that vast accumulation of information, misinformation, and disinformation. It was a treacherous minefield for the unwary, but I was adept at separating fact from fiction. Now that I had a name I might get somewhere.

I typed in "Wolf Creek" and instantly came up with a large number of hits, everything from a ski resort to a film to an amphitheater that all shared the name and had nothing to do with the short-lived village of Wolf Creek near Verona.

I did not give up on my search. I patiently examined the results for a couple of hours without success and then I found something. It was not an earth-shattering discovery and might not be any use at all, but Wolf Creek was mentioned in a list of early Indiana photographers. There was no information about the town, only its name and that of the resident photographer, Theodorus Blackwood.

I remembered the single store that shimmered into existence in Wolf Creek. I had thought it odd that a tiny village like Wolf Creek would have a photography studio, even one that shared space in a dry goods store, but the list was confirmation of the truth. The information was provided by the Indiana Historical Society and therefore could be trusted.

I examined the list more closely. It was arranged by decade and there were only five names listed for the 1840's. Wolf Creek was the only village mentioned north of Indianapolis. The others were in the south.

The clock on my mantle struck midnight. I yawned. I wanted to keep going, but my wits were sleepy. There were times when research was best left for another day. This was one of those times. I put the laptop to sleep, climbed into bed, and closed my eyes wondering if I would dream of Wolf Creek.

Chapter Two

I did not have an opportunity to continue my research the next morning because almost immediately after a breakfast of French toast, bacon, and hot tea in the dining room I received a call from George Madison.

"You're up early. I thought the museum didn't open until ten," I said.

"You know me. I practically live here."

"Did you come up with any additional information on Wolf Creek?"

"Unfortunately, no. I'm calling about another matter. Something strange has occurred. Could you come over later this morning?"

I could tell by George's tone that he was flustered and upset.

"I'll be right there."

A few minutes later I parked the hearse in front of the Verona Historical Society Museum. It was still well before the opening time painted on the glass door, but the sign read "Open." I entered to find George pacing the main exhibit area.

"What happened?" I asked.

"Take a look at this."

George led me to a glass case. Inside were a number of old photographs. I gazed at them, then looked back at George.

"What?"

"Take a close look at the three on the far left."

I moved in and examined the display. On the far left were three miniature photo albums, no more than two inches tall. I had seen such albums before. They held only one small photo, matted with gold behind glass. If I remembered correctly they were designed for carrying in the pocket of a loved one.

"They're early albums, right?"

"Yes, 1840's or 50's."

"I don't see anything strange about them. They're merely empty frames."

"Do you see anyone in the frames?"

I thought the question peculiar. I looked again, although I knew there was no image in any of the three.

"No."

"Each of those albums contained a daguerreotype yesterday; two were of young men, one of an elderly woman."

"Someone stole them? Why?"

"No. That case is always kept locked and I have the only key."

I peered into the case again.

"How could anyone even get the photos out of the frames? The albums are still sealed."

"They didn't remove the photos. The daguerreotypes are still in the frames. It is only the images that are missing. They were there yesterday and this morning they are not."

"You're sure they were there yesterday?"

"Positive. I stopped to look at that display right before I closed up yesterday evening. This morning, as I was making my rounds, I noticed the images were missing."

"That is strange," I said, looking into the case again. I could see upon closer examination that the daguerreotypes were indeed still in the frames. There was even a faint outline of where the images had been.

"There's something else. When I came in this morning the museum felt especially cold and I could swear a chill breeze rushed past me."

I gazed around the interior of the museum. I could see no ghosts except for that of an elderly woman who sat reading in a Victorian armchair. She was always present, content with her book. There were no other spirits about.

I examined the case again. There was no broken glass and no sign of forced entry. Even if there were it would not explain how the images had disappeared right off the photographic plates.

"Could the images have faded out?" I asked.

"No. Photographs printed on paper fade if they are exposed to too much light for too long a period of time, but daguerreotypes don't fade like that and the light level is controlled in all the cases here. Take a look at the other two daguerreotypes. That's what they generally look like."

The images of the remaining daguerreotypes had a mirror-like quality to them and weren't as distinct as the other types of photography on display, but it was quite easy to see the individuals in the photographs.

"I can see why you called me," I said, turning back to George.

"This seemed right up your alley. You're also one of the few who would believe such a story. Others might think I was trying to drum up publicity for the museum. Have you heard of anything like this before?"

"No. I've heard and witnessed accounts of haunted objects, like Matilda over there," I said pointing to the chair, "but I've never heard of an image disappearing out of a photograph."

George could not see her, but I had long ago told him about the old woman in the chair. It had belonged to a woman named Matilda Scroggs and I had identified her in an old family photograph, which is why I knew her name. I could converse with some spirits, but Matilda did not respond whenever I'd tried to speak to her.

"At least you've confirmed I'm not imagining things."

I laughed.

"This is damn peculiar."

"Do you think there is any cause for concern?" George asked. He was right to be cautious after the murder connected to a museum artifact just last month.

"I'm not certain. I would say 'no' but I would have said the same about the surgical instrument case. Most supernatural occurrences are benign, but others are malignant. I suggest caution. Contact me immediately if anything out of the ordinary occurs, even if it seems entirely inconsequential."

"Do you have any idea what happened?"

"Some cultures believe that photography steals the soul. Notable examples are some of the Native Americans as well as the aborigines of Australia. If we accept this as truth then the souls of those in these photographs have escaped. The problem is we don't know if there is any truth to the belief. All we know for sure is that there doesn't seem to be any logical reason for the images to disappear. The supernatural is definitely at work here."

"That is creepy."

"That's the theory that comes to mind. The true explanation may be quite different, but you can be certain I will be working on this. I find it fascinating."

"I thought you might."

"Keep an eye on those photographs and let me know if the images return. I'd like to set up some recording equipment just in case that happens."

"Certainly."

"I'll make a trip to the car. I'll be right back."

I returned soon with a small collection of instruments and cameras. The cameras would record any movement in or around the case, including infrared and other wavelengths the human eye could not detect. The instruments would detect abrupt changes in temperature, electromagnetic activity and so forth. I generally relied on my own developed senses, but sometimes the use of scientific instruments was necessary.

"I've tried to keep everything as inconspicuous as possible. If anyone asks, you can tell them it's motion detecting equipment connected to the burglar alarm. I take it the alarm wasn't set off either."

"No."

"Okay, that's all I can do here. I'll let you know what I find out. Oh, I came up with a name connected to Wolf Creek."

I told George about the list of early photographers and then showed it to him online. He was unfamiliar with the name, but recorded the information to put in his files.

I headed back to Graymoor. Now, I had two mysteries to hopefully solve. The first was certainly the more urgent, but the second also intrigued me. It was at times like this that I especially enjoyed being a paranormal investigator.

I hit the books and the Internet when I returned to The Graymoor Mansion. I had what was perhaps the largest private library of books on the supernatural in existence and had even taken over an entire room to accommodate them. Sean and his parents, who owned the mansion, didn't mind. There were so many rooms it was likely no one had ever been in them all in recent times. Only a part of the mansion had been restored. Vast areas had not been touched since the 19th century.

I spent the rest of the morning in my library, took a short break for a barbeque sandwich and coleslaw for lunch, then went right back to my books.

Images disappearing from photographs must have been an especially rare event because I could not find a single recorded instance. There was no way I could search through all my books, but I knew which ones were the most likely to contain a reference to the phenomena. I checked them all out and—nothing.

The Internet was of no use at all. I obtained plenty of hits, but all were for either fictional events or non-supernatural photography effects. This time, the Internet was useless.

I was making no progress at all with my research so I decided to take a break. I walked downstairs and through the winding hallways until I entered the Natatorium where I expected to find Skye. I was not disappointed. He was back in the weight room, oiling the machines.

"Want to go on a field trip?" I asked.

"Did a new voodoo shop open?"

"Funny Skye. Actually, I want to check out Wolf Creek in the light of day. I'm not expecting any trouble, but I could use some backup."

"Oh yeah. Colin told me about your adventure last night. Why don't you go to the movies like a normal person?"

"Because I'm not normal."

"You'll get no argument from me. Okay, I'm in, but I'm driving."

I followed Skye outside to the old carriage house he used as a garage for his Skyemobile, a 1935 Auburn boattail speedster. Skye loved the car even more than I did my hearse. The Auburn certainly cost more. One could buy a nice house for less than he'd paid for that automobile.

"So, fill me in. Colin told me about a ghost village and being chased by ghosts. It sounds like you had a good time last night."

I told Skye the tale, stopping only to give him directions. I hadn't finished by the time we pulled into the abandoned drive. We hopped out of the car and continued on foot while I brought him up to speed.

"Here we are," I said as we reached the meadow.

"This is it? Wow, I'm so glad I came."

"I told you there wasn't much physical evidence left, smartass."

"You weren't kidding. I don't see anything."

I pointed to the ruins of the well.

"So what are we seeking?"

"I'm not sure. Probably nothing. I mainly want to get a good look at this place in the daylight now that I've seen the phantom version.

"The dry goods store was about here," I said, walking to an area several yards away.

I stomped around in the tall grass for a couple of minutes while Skye looked at me as if I'd gone insane.

"Yeah, here's the foundation. This was the dry goods store and photography shop."

"Photography shop? I thought you said the village was here in the 1840's."

"I did. Photography dates back a little earlier than that."

"Ah okay, what a weird mix in a shop."

"Not really. The store may well have also acted as the post office, doctor's office, barber, and dentist for all we know. It wasn't uncommon back then. Go far enough back in time and your barber would have also been your dentist and perhaps surgeon."

"I'll stay in the present then, thank you very much."

Skye followed me as I examined the site, but he looked rather bored. Skye was accustomed to considerably more excitement, more than most would believe.

"The foundations match what I witnessed last night," I said.

"Was there any doubt?"

"Some phantom structures have been known to move. There is a farmhouse in Illinois that has been sighted several times along one road, but not always in the same place. These spectral structures are appearing where the actual structures once stood."

I rubbed my chin. This was a real puzzle. I stood there for some time trying to figure out what was going on in this place.

"Marshall, we have company and I don't think they're from our time period," Skye said, breaking into my thoughts.

I turned. Skye was correct. The figures were indistinct in the light of day, but I could make out enough detail to see they were wearing clothing from a hundred and fifty years ago. They fit the descriptions of the ghosts who attacked Tor and Riley.

"Damn!" Skye said as the village shimmered into existence around us. "Now this is more like it!"

I turned quickly, trying to take in as much as possible while the specters were still distant. The structures wavered from completely transparent to almost solid and back again. I could make out much more detail in the light of day and tried to commit everything to memory while I had the chance.

The pair of ghosts moved quickly toward us.

"What's the plan?" Skye asked calmly. That's one of the things I loved about Skye; nothing rattled him.

"I think a strategic withdrawal is in order. I don't think there is anything to be gained by confronting this pair. All I'm reading from them is anger."

"That may not be so easy," Skye said, looking to this right.

More specters had appeared. One was an old woman wielding what looked like a scythe. The other was a young man with a butcher knife.

I looked behind us. A young boy holding an ax grinned at us manically.

"It's definitely time to leave. Go!"

We ran for the gap between the old woman and the boy. All the ghosts converged on us quickly. The young man near the old woman cut us off so I dug into my pocket as I ran and pulled out a handful of salt. As he raised his butcher knife to strike I hurled the salt toward him and he vaporized. The boy was almost upon us, but Skye drew a dagger he had concealed somewhere on him and slashed at the boy, obliterating him. Neither of the murderous specters were gone for good. One could not kill what was already dead, but they were temporarily disabled.

We broke into a sprint. Skye could easily outrun me, but he remained at my side, ever watchful and prepared to act. We jumped in the Auburn. Skye started it up, slammed it in reverse, and hit the gas. In seconds we were headed back toward town.

"I wasn't expecting that in full daylight," Skye said.

"Ghosts are limited to coming out at night only in fiction," I said.

"At least things livened up near the end. I was getting bored."

"So you prefer ghosts who are out to kill you to boredom? Wait. Don't answer that. I already know what you're going to say."

Skye gave me a cocky grin.

"I'm surprised you didn't want to stay and have a chat with them. That is your usual thing," Skye said.

"Those ghosts were not in a talking mood. The only thing I sensed from them was hostility and malevolence."

"That kid was a scary little shit." I laughed. "Why didn't you sense them when we arrived?" Skye asked.

"They weren't there. I didn't sense them until the moment you spotted them. They may have been near or perhaps our presence caused them to materialize. It's hard to say. I believe they are tied to that spot, but I can't even be sure of that. I've never seen a haunting quite like this."

"That should make you happy then."

"It would if they weren't trying to kill everyone who visits their village."

"Yeah, that's gonna hurt tourism for sure. What?" Skye said when I gave him my annoyed look.

"These ghosts are dangerous, Skye."

"Yeah, I gathered that when junior wanted to chop me with his ax. You're the expert. How do we get rid of them?"

"I could salt the entire site, but that would only be a temporary solution. The first time it rained it would likely wash the salt away. We could stake the remains, if we could find them."

"Stake the remains? Isn't that a vampire thing?"

"You know that does not work on vampires."

"Yeah, but it does on ghosts?"

"Sort of."

"What do you mean sort of?"

"It's impossible to kill a spirit, but just as slashing or stabbing one with metal will temporarily disintegrate it, staking the remains with metal will obliterate the ghost for as long as the metal lasts. It's a long term, but not permanent solution."

"I'll take your word for it."

"It's rather impractical. There is a graveyard near the village, but we'd have to dig up the whole damn thing and stake each body, if we could find them. Most of the graves aren't marked and what's left might not be recognizable as human remains and some of the ghosts may be buried elsewhere."

"I see your point. You do have unique problems, Marshall. You can count me in, of course. If you want to visit the village again I'll bring my sword."

"Oh yeah, any excuse to use the sword."

"Hell yeah!" Skye said.

We returned to the mansion. Skye headed for the Natatorium and I went to my room upstairs. I had investigated plenty of hauntings, but never one like this. I was intrigued, but even more concerned for the safety of anyone who was unfortunate enough to walk through the ruins of Wolf Creek.

***

"I have a case for you," Agent Heck said when I answered my cell.

"Another murder in a locked room?" I asked, referring to a recent series of murders I'd helped solve.

"No, this one is even more bizarre. There are three witnesses that swear that a ghost stepped out of a photograph and beat the victim to death with a wooden maul."

"I'm interested," I said.

"I thought you might be. How far are you from Grass Creek, Indiana?"

"Hmm, maybe half an hour."

"I'll arrange for you to have access to the crime scene. I'm there now. Will you be bringing your partner?"

I smiled at what Skye would think of being called my partner."

"Yes, if I can."

"I'll arrange access for both of you."

"I'll get there as soon as possible."

"I'll have copies of the crime scene photos, witness testimony, and all other pertinent documents sent to you."

I left my room and walked downstairs as we continued to talk. I had nearly reached the Natatorium by the time we finished. I entered to find Skye swimming laps. I stood at the end of the pool so he would see me. He stopped when he reached my end.

"What's up?"

"The F.B.I. called."

"Your past finally caught up with you, huh?"

"Funny. It was Agent Heck. Someone was murdered in Grass Creek by a spirit that emerged from a photograph. Interested in going with me? I'm departing as soon as possible."

Skye hoisted himself out of the pool. He was wearing only a skimpy blue Speedo. Water cascaded over his defined muscular body. Skye was gorgeous. It was no wonder so many found him irresistibly attractive.

"I'll change and be right out," he said, grabbing a towel and heading for the locker room.

"Good, because I'm not taking you if you're going to wear that."

Skye laughed.

The Natatorium was one of the most beautiful parts of The Graymoor Mansion. Chilly autumn rain pelted down onto the glass roof and ran down the glass walls in rivulets, but inside the Natatorium was pleasantly warm. A hint of chorine scented the air and the blue water glowed from the lights in the pool. The large plants placed among the marble statues almost made me feel as if I was in a jungle.

"I'm ready," Skye said, emerging almost impossibly soon dressed in khaki, pants, a blue plaid button down shirt, and jacket.

"How do you change so quickly? No, don't answer that." Skye smiled. "Let's be off to exciting Grass Creek."

"I don't think exciting has ever been used in a sentence with Grass Creek before. I've driven through there. It makes Verona look like Los Angeles."

"There has been a murder. It will be exciting today."

I drove along the county highways south of Verona. It was a mostly wild area with lots of trees and a few farms. I knew we were getting close when we came to the hairpin turns where the road followed old field boundaries.

There truly wasn't much in Grass Creek, beyond several homes, an abandoned feed store, and an old train station. The town, if it could be called that, was nearly deserted.

"Now we know where everyone is," Skye said as we rounded a corner and arrived at our destination. There was quite a crowd gathered beyond a turn-of-the-century home. Two sheriffs' vehicles were parked in the drive and an ambulance was pulled up to the front door.

A sheriff's deputy stopped us at the door until we flashed our F.B.I. IDs. We weren't actually working for the F.B.I. on this case, but I figured it would speed things up. Besides, it felt really cool and impressed the onlookers. This was probably the most exciting thing to happen in Grass Creek ever. The deputy walked inside with us.

The interior was filled with antiques, and I mean *filled*. It was so crowded with old furniture and bric-a-brac that a path had been cleared for the gurney. We stepped off to the side as a body was wheeled past us in a bag.

"Show me the photo," I said.

The deputy led us to the side of the room where a number of old photographs were displayed.

"This is it," the deputy said, handing it to me.

"It's a daguerreotype," I said looking at Skye.

It was an album holding a single photo, like those in the museum in Verona, only larger. It featured an Empire period rocking chair in front of black curtains. No one was pictured in the photo.

"The witnesses said a young man came out of that photo and bludgeoned Mrs. Curry to death. Can you believe it?" the deputy asked.

"As a matter of fact, I can."

He looked truly surprised.

I examined the album more closely. On the opposite side from the photo was an inscription, bordered in black. Printed lettering read, "In Memoriam, Thomas Jenkins, 1818 – 1842."

"In Memoriam?" Skye asked.

"It's Latin. It means, 'In Memory Of.' It's often used in epitaphs on grave markers and on memorial items like this."

I recorded the inscription in my notebook.

"Are the witnesses still here?"

"Yes, the sheriff is finishing up his questioning."

"Take us to them please."

He led us into the adjoining room. The sheriff was just closing up his pad.

"Skye Mackenzie, F.B.I. This is my associate, Marshall Mulgrew," Skye said, burying himself in the part. I shot him a look, but he only raised his eyebrows.

"We'd like to ask your witnesses a few questions," I said.

The sheriff pulled us into the other room.

"You can ask them anything you want, but they're talking crazy. I think one or maybe all of them did it."

We walked back into the room where three elderly ladies sat.

"Can you tell us what happened?"

"We already told the sheriff. He doesn't believe us and who could blame him," said one.

"Try me."

"We were sitting in the living room, chatting, when a young man emerged from a photo and attacked Minnie. He killed her before we could even think of trying to save her, not that we could have. He was a strong young man. I'm ashamed to admit that we ran screaming from the house."

"That's probably the wisest thing you could have done at that point. It may have saved your lives."

The women looked at me with surprised expressions on their faces.

"I believe your story. This isn't the first time someone has emerged from a photo, although you're the first who have witnessed it happen."

The women looked at each other as if they couldn't believe what I was saying.

"I'm afraid the sheriff will charge us with murder," one of the ladies said.

"If he does, I think the prosecutor will drop the case as soon as he reads my reports. What can you tell me about the photo? We're attempting to figure out what is going on before someone else dies."

"Not much, except that Minnie bought it at an auction a few years ago. She's always buying things at auction, she *was*."

The women grew emotional.

"Do you know where it was purchased?" I asked.

"It was a community consignment auction, but I don't know where."

"Can you describe the man who committed the murder?"

I listened carefully and made notes, although none of the ladies had remained in the room long enough to get a good look at the murderer. I doubted his appearance or clothing would help me figure out what was happening, but sometimes seemingly tiny details were the key.

"Okay, thank you very much ladies," I said when they'd told me as much about the murderer as they could, which wasn't much.

"That's it?" Skye asked as we walked back through the house.

"That's all that pertains to our case," I said.

We walked back out to the hearse, which was attracting quite a bit of attention. We climbed in and headed back to Verona.

"I hoped to discover more, but the photo is from the same time period as the others. I have a feeling more murders will follow."

"So that poor woman was killed just because she bought an old photograph at an auction?"

"That seems to be the case."

"First, the Mad Hatter case. Now, this. Remind me to never start a collection."

"Ah, come on, Skye. I thought you lived for danger."

"Excitement maybe. Danger? No."

"So you don't want to start a daguerreotype collection?"

"Even if I was interested in old photos of people I don't know, which I'm not, I think the possibility that one of them might come out of the photo and try to kill me would dampen my enthusiasm."

"I'm going to see if I can find out anything about Thomas Jenkins. Most such photos are unmarked. Doing so was unnecessary because whoever owned the photographs knew who was pictured in them. Since this one was a memorial photo we may have caught a break or the name may be no help at all."

"I would help you with that research, but... I don't want to."

I laughed.

"I appreciate your honesty."

"It is way too boring, but I am up for being chased by murderous ghosts anytime."

"Good, because I plan to return to Wolf Creek sooner or later and I'd like to have you along."

"I'll bring my sword."

"Any excuse to whip out the sword huh?"

"I'll ignore the double-entendre. It's far more useful than a dagger."

"Which you just happened to have on you during our last visit."

"I'm always prepared. I would have made a kick-ass Boy Scout."

"I can't picture you as a Boy Scout. You're more of an Anti-Scout."

"Me?" Skye asked, as innocently as possible, which wasn't effective in the least.

Half an hour later I was back in my room and on my laptop. When I searched for "Thomas Jenkins" online I came up with an enormous number of hits, but not one that was useful. I tried searching for the name combined with the year of his birth and death, but that brought up no useful results either. I was not surprised, but it was worth a shot.

I spent the remainder of my day with my books, researching occurrences of phantom structures and spirits emerging from photographs or paintings. There were quite a few references to phantom structures, but none for an entire village. As for spirits emerging from objects, I came up with nothing. Ghosts were quite often associated with objects. It was not unusual for a spirit to watch over a favorite desk, painting, bed or other item, such as the elderly lady who sat in the Victorian chair in the Verona Historical Society Museum. I couldn't come up with any instance of a spirit associated with an item doing harm. I felt as if I'd reached a dead end on both cases.

Chapter Three

"Marshall, can you come to the shop, right now please?" Sean's mom, Kayla, asked as soon as I answered the phone. I could tell from the tone of her voice she was frightened.

"I'll be right there."

I hurried downstairs and to the carriage house where I kept my hearse beside Skye's Auburn. I quickly drove the short distance to Graymoor Antiques downtown.

I found Kayla standing outside of her shop, holding her cell phone and pacing.

"What's wrong?" I asked as soon as I emerged from the car. I knew it had to be something serious. Sean's mom had lived in The Graymoor Mansion for years. She was not spooked by the average supernatural occurrence or anything else for that matter.

"Sean told me about the woman murdered by a spirit that came out of a photograph. It happened here just before I called you as I was eating my lunch. I saw it come out of the photograph and come toward me. I opened the salt shaker, threw the salt at it and ran outside."

I smiled. Kayla Hilton knew a thing or two about ghosts. One did not live in The Graymoor Mansion for long without learning a few things about the supernatural.

"Wait in my car while I check this out. You'll be safe there. Spirits cannot enter the hearse."

I entered the shop, which was located in an old brick store building not far from the museum. I grabbed a sword that was on display in the window just in case the spirit was in a bad mood and was lingering in the shop.

I spotted Kayla's unfinished lunch on the counter. Moments later I located the photograph. It was a daguerreotype like the others, housed in a single-photo album. This was the largest I'd seen yet. It measured about four inches by five inches. This one was different in a more significant way as well. There were still people in the photo, two of them, a middle-age man and woman. The man had his arm around someone who was no longer there.

I sensed a ghost in the shop, but it was not malicious. It was the spirit of an old woman who gazed at a Hoosier cabinet and then around the shop with a perplexed expression on her face.

Here was a spirit attached to an object, in her case a kitchen cabinet that dated to about 1900.

"The cabinet isn't in your home anymore," I said.

She looked at me as if seeing me for the first time. Many spirits were lost in their own little world until someone with the ability reached out to them.

"You're dead. Your cabinet has passed into the hands of another, but don't worry, she'll take good care of it. Cabinets like yours are highly sought after now. It will be fine. You don't have to worry about it. You can go and be with your family."

She smiled for the barest instant and then disappeared, leaving the shop vacant of spirits. I went back outside and opened the door of my hearse.

"It's okay. He's not in there and I don't think he'll return. None of the spirits who emerged from photos have come back, but we can salt the shop to be sure."

I opened the back of the hearse and pulled out one of my bags. I always kept a large supply of salt on hand.

Immediately upon entering the shop I placed a narrow line of salt around the borders of the shop, hiding it under the rug by the door so customers entering wouldn't disturb it. I removed the daguerreotypes from the shelf, lifted the cloth under them and created a ring of salt under it before replacing the cloth and photographs.

"Okay. Now you're safe. The spirit can't get back in and if any spirit comes out of another photograph it will be trapped."

"Thank you, Marshall."

I gazed at the remaining four photographs. Something was off about them. I picked up first one and then another to examine them more closely. One was of a toddler seated in a chair; another was of two young boys, another a group of children, and the last was of a young woman leaning on an older woman on a sofa. I looked back at Kayla after I had examined all four.

"These are poste mortem photographs," I said.

"You have a good eye. Most people don't know unless I tell them."

"The photo from which the spirit emerged was one too, wasn't it?" I asked.

"Yes. There was a boy of about fifteen seated between his parents. I don't actually like those photos very much. They're so sad. I bought them with a lot of other photographs at an auction long ago. I only dug them out recently."

"I wonder... Do you think you'll be okay now?" I asked.

"Yes, thank you very much, Marshall."

"Thank you. You've given me an idea."

I left Kayla's shop and walked the short distance to the museum. George was giving a couple a tour. I waited until he finished and left them on their own to browse.

"What can I do for you Marshall?"

"I have a question. Were the photographs we discussed recently poste mortem photos?" I asked, not saying more than was necessary since those touring the museum could hear us.

"Yes. Yes, they were. I didn't think to mention it. Is it important?"

"I'm not sure, but possibly. Thank you. That's all I needed to know."

I departed, then drove back to the mansion. Upon my arrival, I pulled out my cell phone and called Sean. It was a much faster way of locating him than searching for him in the mansion. He told me I'd find him in the kitchen, waiting while Martha fixed him a pot of tea.

As I walked into the kitchen I said to Sean: "I need to talk."

"Good timing. I'm about to take a break. Let me grab another cup."

Martha handed him a second cup, as well as a plate of cookies, before he could move toward the cupboard. Sean placed them on the tray and carried it from the kitchen. We walked out into the lobby and then down a hallway until we reached a small private dining room. It was furnished in Victorian antiques, like all of Graymoor. I particularly liked this dining room. It had a small table with two large, ornate Belter chairs. I always felt as if I was sitting on a throne when I sat in one.

I waited until Sean put the tray down before I spoke.

"I just came from your mom's shop."

"Have you started collecting antiques?"

"Why would I need to collect them? I'm surrounded by them. Everything in Graymoor is antique."

Sean laughed.

"You mom called and asked me to come to the shop. She's fine, but she was attacked by a ghost."

"What?"

I recounted the tale for Sean and told him about the precautions I'd taken to insure his mom's safety.

"I truly don't believe he will return, but if he does he won't be able to enter the store. Your mother is rather good at taking care of herself too. She kicked that ghost's butt by throwing salt at him."

Sean laughed.

"Should I call her?"

"She's fine. She'll probably tell you all about it when she gets home."

I took a sip of tea. I was pretty sure it was Yorkshire. The cookies were chocolate chip, one of my favorites.

"I did discover something interesting in your mom's shop. The photo the spirit emerged from was poste mortem."

"What's that?"

"It's Latin. It means, 'after death.'"

"Well, wouldn't it have to be since it's so old?"

"No, poste mortem means a photo taken after death. In other words, it's a picture taken of someone after they have died."

"Why the hell would anyone want something like that?"

"It was more a matter of necessity than desire. We can grab a digital camera or pull out our phones and take a hundred photos and think nothing of it, but in the nineteenth century, almost no one outside of professional photographers and the very rich owned a camera. Photographs were expensive. That's why a family photo was such a huge deal in the past. When someone died, especially a child, there likely were no photos of them. If the family wanted a photo for remembrance, it had to be taken after they died."

"I still wouldn't want one. That's just too creepy. I'd rather try to remember them as they were."

"I don't like poste mortem photographs myself."

"I would have thought photos of dead people would be right up your alley."

134

"I'm not bothered by the dead in the photos, except when they are children because it's so sad, but by the others. The photos were almost always taken soon after death. The expressions on the faces of the living are filled with sadness and grief. Poste mortem photographs can be very disturbing."

"I suppose that is true."

"When your mom confirmed that the spirit emerged from a poste mortem photograph, I went to the museum and inquired. Those photos were poste mortems too."

"Do you think that's significant?"

"It's a pattern at least, but it also makes the situation more confusing."

"More confusing than ghosts coming out of photos?"

"The generally held belief among some groups is that photography steals the soul, or in other words, the spirit. In the Victorian era, mirrors were covered during funerals because it was believed that the spirit of the dead could become trapped in a mirror."

"That's crazy."

"I'm not saying I believe either is true, but a spirit emerging from a poste mortem photograph makes little sense because the spirit would have already left the body before the photo could be taken."

"So, if photography does steal the soul, a spirit emerging from a photo of a corpse still doesn't make sense. You do have interesting problems to figure out," Sean said.

"I guess I'll fall back on Sherlock Holmes. 'When one eliminates the impossible, whatever remains, however improbable, must be the truth.'"

"Which means?"

"In this case it means that although I find the idea of spirits rising from a photo of the dead improbable and even illogical, that must be what is occurring. We know the spirits are coming out of the photos. All are poste mortem photographs, with the possible exception of the one involved with the Grass Creek murder, but I'm willing to bet that was poste mortem too."

"So to prevent more murders, all you have to do is gather all the poste mortem photos in the world and surround them by a ring of salt."

"While that solution would work, it's impossible. There have to be thousands of them, probably tens of thousands and it's not always possible to tell if a photo is poste mortem."

"I would think it would be very easy to tell."

"Some photographers were so adept at making the dead look lifelike that they do indeed look alive."

"I'm going to sleep well now. There are plenty of old photographs in Graymoor. Some of them could be of dead people."

"It's quite possible."

"Why can't you have a normal job, Marshall, something that won't keep me up at night?"

"You expect me to have a normal job?"

"True and if you weren't a supernatural investigator, who they gonna call?"

"Yeah, like I haven't heard *that* recently."

"Come on, Doctor Venkman. Where's your sense of humor?"

"Shut up and eat your cookie, Sean."

"Do you have any idea of how to stop the murders?"

"Not a clue, but I'll keep working on it."

"You'll figure it out, Marshall. If you can solve a string of murders that occurred in rooms securely locked from the inside, you can do anything."

"Let's hope you're right."

Sean and I sat, talked, and finished off the tea and cookies. Sometimes the best way to come up with a solution to a problem was not to think about it, but I feared this was not one of those times.

***

"We found something," George said as soon as I answered the phone.

"What?"

"It's a journal, written by Theodorus Blackwood. I browsed through it and I think you'll find some of the entries from 1844 extremely interesting."

"I'll be right over."

Finally. Forward movement. I had spent a rather unproductive morning researching obscure beliefs about the soul and about poste mortem photography. Lunch in the dining room improved my mood, but did nothing to help me solve the case. Maybe now I could get somewhere.

The bells rang on the door of the museum as I entered. A volunteer was leading a group of school children on a guided tour. I caught sight of an extra child in the group, a boy who was obviously from another era. I gazed at him until he turned to look at me. He was dressed in knickers, a linen shirt, and a flat cap like those worn in the 1910's and '20's. He smiled at me. He knew I could see him. I nodded and moved on. He did not need my help. He knew he was dead and was where he wanted to be—with other children.

"Marshall," George said, beckoning to me.

I followed George into the back room.

"One of our volunteers discovered this in the archive," he said handing me a thick leather-bound tome with a red ribbon sewn into the binding as a marker. I opened the book to the marked page. "Read the entry for October 14, 1844."

I quickly found the date on the page and read the hand-written entry below.

"The curse Sarah Thornberry laid upon Wolf Creek has wasted no time in coming to pass. Two nights ago, Thomas Newberry was heard screaming for help in his cabin, crying out that Sarah had come for him. We believed he had gone mad but when we entered... Thomas was dead, his face as white as if he'd seen a ghost."

I looked up.

"It gets better. I looked up Sarah Thornberry and Thomas Newberry. I found nothing on Thomas, but I found a reference to Sarah in our genealogical records. The entry read, "Sarah Thornberry, Born June 6, 1774, Died October 12, 1844, executed – witch."

"Witch?"

George nodded. I returned to the journal. The words, "second murder" caught my eye.

"Last night, the village was awakened by screams yet again, this time coming from the home of Patience Elwood. Those of us

who rushed to her aide heard her call out, 'Thomas! No!' and when we entered, we saw Thomas Newberry with his hands around her throat. We rushed him, but he was not there. It was his ghost and we could do nothing as he squeezed the life out of Patience.

"I have little doubt that Sarah is coming for all those who accused her and caused her to be burned alive."

"Oh my God. How could this have happened *here*? They burned her."

"Apparently Wolf Creek is our own little Salem, Massachusetts," George said.

"Fools."

"It's a part of Verona's history we knew nothing about."

"Where and when was this journal obtained?" I asked.

"We have no idea, but it was in a box with other unrelated items that hadn't been unpacked since the museum moved to this location in the 1980's. Apparently, no one thought it especially significant when it was donated or purchased. The early entries are rather mundane until they get into his photography. If we hadn't been searching for the name, who knows how long it would have been before we realized the significance of the journal."

"I need to study this," I said.

"If you promise to guard it well you can take it with you. No one else would be allowed, but I understand the urgency of this matter."

"Thank you, George."

George wrapped the journal in tissue paper and then boxed it for transport.

"I'll take good care of it and will return it as soon as possible," I said.

"I can't wait until you do. I'm eager to study it myself."

I returned to my room in the mansion with my treasure. I would have found the journal intriguing even without a case attached to it. While I found the idea of a witch burning disturbing, I also found it fascinating. In the famous Salem witch trials, many innocent people were killed in an uncontrolled plague of opportunism, fear, and religious fervor, but quite likely

Sarah Thornberry actually was a witch. Even so, I did not condone her burning.

The villagers of Wolf Creek brought their fate on themselves and I had little sympathy for them, but the murder victims of the present did not deserve to die.

I began reading the journal of Theodorus Blackwood from the very beginning so as not to miss anything. Most of the early entries were rather uninteresting for the most part, but told a tale of Theodorus struggling to earn an income with photography equipment he had purchased used with hard earned money from his work in a flourmill.

My interest heightened at the first mention of Sarah Thornberry; *"I chastised the children and chased them away for tormenting Sarah Thornberry as she walked to her home beyond the edge of the village, but did not dare to attempt to befriend her for I had heard she shunned all but the most necessary contact with others. Some thought her a witch, but that did not stop them from going to her for cures in times of illness."*

The words of Theodorus rang true. Far in the past more than one old woman who used herbs as medicine was suspected of being a witch by the ignorant. Such women were misunderstood and generally feared. It was a familiar, sad story.

The journal was most concerned with everyday life in Wolf Creek and the successes and failures of Theodorus as a photographer. George would most certainly be mesmerized by the account. While I found it intriguing, my interest was fired each time Sarah Thornberry was mentioned. She popped up now and again, often when Theodorus recorded some secret act of kindness he performed for her, such as leaving food at her cabin door in the dead of night. The more I read, the more my fondness for Theodorus grew. He seemed like a voice of wisdom and reason in a village of ignorance and suspicion.

I came upon an entry about a missing child, a girl, who went missing three days before Sarah was burned as a witch. Suspicion immediately fell upon Sarah, and despite lack of evidence she was almost universally condemned as the cause of the girl's disappearance. It was this disappearance that finally turned the villagers on her. She was burned alive and then the murders began.

The entry of October 16, 1844 proved Sarah's innocence; *"Ginny Smith wandered into town, exhausted, starved, and disoriented, but alive. Wolf Creek sentenced an innocent woman to her death. Of that there is no question because her assumed victim now walks the streets of Wolf Creek and Sarah lies unburied on the hill outside of the village. Wolf Creek deserves to be cursed and yet I would stop the killings of my friends and neighbors if I could."*

The following entries were a grisly account of more murders and the departure of two families from Wolf Creek. Then, came another I found of special interest.

"The village buried Sarah Thornberry yesterday in an effort to appease her, but last night there was another murder. Perhaps if they had buried her in good conscience her spirit would have relented, but still they cling to their hatred and beliefs and refused to bury her in the churchyard, instead burying her near where she was burned.

"Sarah obviously was a witch. I know that now, but I cannot help but think that the fault lies with those who accused and condemned her. Sarah did no harm to anyone until after she was burned to death for a crime she did not commit. Who can blame her for seeking her revenge?

I made a list of the victims and anyone else mentioned in the journal, but there was no need to search for a pattern. Sarah began with her main accusers and worked her way out. More individuals and families fled Wolf Creek, but I did not know if it saved them or if Sarah's vengeful spirit pursued them. After the first murder, Sarah herself did not appear, or if she did it was not recorded. Instead, she called forth the recent dead to punish those who yet lived.

I took a break for supper. Skye, Colin, and Sean were seated together so I joined them with my plate of baked chicken, dressing, mashed potatoes and cranberry sauce.

"I thought you'd disappeared," Skye said.

"I've been in my room most of the day, reading Theodorus Blackwood's journal."

I gave the guys the short version of what I'd discovered.

"I knew a witch would come into our lives sooner or later. It was only a matter of time. Wait until Thad hears about this. He'll want a copy of that journal. I bet he can get a novel out of it," Skye said.

Thad T. Thomas was a one-time romantic interest of Skye's and a well-known occult writer. He visited The Graymoor Mansion upon occasion, mostly to pick up new material for books.

"You think the present murders are due to an 1844 curse?" Sean asked.

"I don't see how, although I can't know for sure. I'd have to know the nature of the curse to even make a guess and only Sarah Thornberry has that information."

"You could ask her," Skye said.

"Absolutely not!" Sean said.

"I have to agree. I know very little about witches. Attempting to contact her would be far too dangerous."

"What's life without a little danger?" Colin asked.

"Contacting a witch wouldn't be a little dangerous, it would be extremely dangerous. Besides, I don't think there's a connection unless the present day victims are descendants of those who killed Sarah Thornberry."

"Do you think that likely?" Skye asked.

"My instinct tells me it isn't. Something else is going on here. There may be no connection between what's happening now and what happened in 1844. The dead came forth to murder in both times, but in 1844 they came out of their graves. Now, they're coming out of photographs."

"So what's your next step?" Sean asked.

"Read the rest of Theodorus's journal and then see what else I can dig up."

"Grave robbing?" Skye asked with a smirk.

"No, dumb ass."

"I thought maybe it could be a new side business for you."

"I think not. Let's talk about something else. How is wrestling, Colin?"

"I am undefeated so far. I figure first I'll break Skye's old records and then go after Ethan Selby's."

"I think you have a good shot at beating mine, but to beat Ethan's you'll have to go undefeated from now on," Skye said.

"That is a bit of a challenge, but then again we are talking about me here," Colin said, standing and stretching to reveal his impossibly defined abdomen.

"You have spent way too much time around your uncle," I said.

"Don't blame me. He was like this when I got him," Skye said.

"Maybe it's genetic," Sean said.

"Yeah, it's the superior Mackenzie genes," Skye said.

"Uh huh," Sean said.

"Hey, where's Nick anyway?" I asked. "I haven't seen him in a while."

"You haven't seen him because you've been holed up in your room. He was here less than an hour ago," Sean said.

"I guess I have spent a lot of time on research. Speaking of which, I need to get back to it."

I stopped by the kitchen after I left the dining room and asked Martha for a pot of tea. I had the feeling my evening might stretch all the way until tomorrow morning.

A few minutes later I headed upstairs with my Yorkshire tea. I poured myself a cup and continued reading the journal of Theodorus Blackwood.

The pages of the journal recounted more murders and more departures from Wolf Creek by those who decided to get out while they could. Then, came a different entry.

"I photographed the Jarvis boy today at his home. His parents wanted a remembrance of him before they buried him in the ground, never to see him again. This was the first time I attempted to photograph the dead and we only managed by Mr. and Mrs. Jarvis sitting on either side of their dead ten-year-old son, with Mr. Jarvis supporting his head by placing his arm over his son's shoulders. I do not know how the grieving parents could bare to sit there while the plate was exposed. I had to hide my own tears so as not to add to their grief."

I had never thought about a poste mortem photo from the photographer's perspective. It was upsetting and disturbing to even view such photos. It must have been horrible to actually be there while one was taken and what of the poor parents?

"It has been three days since the Jarvis boy was buried and he has not risen to attack the living like the others. Why?"

I pondered that myself.

I continued with my grim reading as thunder began to rumble in the distance. Lightning soon joined the thunder and within minutes cold rain pounded against the windowpanes. A chill began to pervade the room so I lit a fire. It helped to dispel the chill and the gloom, but it was still a rather Edgar Allen Poe night.

Theodorus wrote of another poste mortem photograph and then noted with great interest that the subject of the photo did not rise from the dead. My thoughts were echoed by the next entry.

"Twice now the dead have remained in their grave after I have photographed them. Is this cause and effect?

"Three times in the past I have asked some of the rare few Indians who still reside in the area to photograph them and each time have been refused. One old woman said she did not wish to be photographed because the image would steal her soul. I thought that ridiculous, but respected her wishes. Now, I wonder if her belief was true. Did photography capture some part of the spirit or soul? Was that why the dead I photographed did not return to trouble the living?"

My phone rang, causing me to jump.

"Marshall, it's Agent Heck. There has been another murder and we have a witness who says a ghost came out of a photograph and killed his brother. I'm on the scene now."

"Just like the Grass Creek murder."

"That's why I called."

"Where?"

"Charleston, South Carolina."

"Damn. Can you describe the photograph to me?"

"It's old, like the one at Grass Creek, a daguerreotype. There are two teens in the photo, but between them there is only a sort of stand."

"One that could be used to hold a body in place?"

"Yes. The witness said there were three teen boys in that photograph."

"He's telling the truth," I said.

"I believe so too. That's why we're not holding him for murder."

"Is there anything else unusual about the photograph?"

"No, but the facing page contains three locks of hair and three names."

"Give me the names."

I wrote each down as Agent Heck read them off to me.

"Got it. I think I may be onto something. I need to check it out further, but I think I know what's going on now."

I told Agent Heck my suspicions.

"That's crazy, but I'm growing rather accustomed to crazy."

I laughed.

"I'll keep you informed. Thanks."

We disconnected. I turned to my notes. Nothing. None of the names matched those I had recorded, but perhaps it didn't matter. Theodorus and I were onto something.

I kept reading grim accounts of more murders and more departures from Wolf Creek. Theodorus began to offer his services free of charge to photograph the recent dead. Most accepted and for the first time the murder rate declined. Then, I found a match.

"I photographed Elmer Hutchinson today and it was most difficult. I knew everyone in Wolf Creek, but Elmer shared my interest in photography and spent a good deal of time with me. He was murdered last night, only a week short of his sixteenth birthday. I photographed him using a stand of my own devising. He appeared eerily alive as he stood between his brothers, Bert and Charles. It was the most difficult photograph I have ever taken and I could not stop my tears. Even so, I am glad the family agreed to the photo because I cannot bear the thought of Elmer rising from his grave to kill. He was a kind and gentle soul and would never have wanted that. I am convinced now that only my camera stands between Wolf Creek and total destruction."

I was glad that Theodorus was not alive to learn that Elmer had come back from the dead to murder over a hundred and fifty years after he was buried in the ground.

I continued reading and taking notes until I fell asleep at my desk as the sun began to rise. I did not awaken until past noon, but I knew now what I had to do.

Chapter Four

"I need your help and you get to bring your sword," I said, as I walked into the Natatorium where Skye was setting out more towels.

"Oh, then I am in."

I grinned.

"I'd like Colin to come too, if it's okay with you. It will be dangerous."

"Dangerous how?"

"I need to return to Wolf Creek and if my theory is correct, it's probably crawling with spirits with the urge to kill."

"Lovely."

"Let me bring you up to speed. In 1844, a photographer named Theodorus Blackwood remained in Wolf Creek to battle murderous spirits with his camera."

"With his camera?"

"Yes. Remember what I said about some groups believing that photographs capture the soul?"

"Sure."

"It sounds crazy, but there is truth to it. Theodorus began taking poste mortem photographs of victims. Anyone he photographed did not return to trouble the living. He actually managed to convince the residents of Wolf Creek that he could put a stop to the murders by photographing the dead. Near the end, those who remained began digging up graves so that the corpses could be photographed."

"Sounds like a fun time. So this worked?"

"Yes. The murders at last came to an end, but by then it was too late to save the town. So many had been lost or had fled that there were too few for the village to be viable. A handful remained for a few years, but eventually everyone left and the village was all but forgotten."

"How does this connect to the present?"

"One of the poste mortem photographs involved in a recent murder was one of those taken by Theodorus Blackwood back in 1844. I'm willing to bet that every single photograph involved in murders the last few weeks was taken in Wolf Creek."

"And why are these spooks coming back out of the photos now?"

"That's a good question and I don't have an answer, but I believe those spirits are all returning to Wolf Creek. That's why the village itself is reappearing. We need to recapture the spirits."

"How?"

"Isn't it obvious? We need to take some pictures."

"What about the spirits that have yet to emerge from photographs?"

"That's the difficult part. I need to confront the witch."

"I thought we agreed that was bad."

"Oh, it is, but the alternative is that more people die. There are more murders to come. I'm also not sure how long the photos can hold the spirits. If we don't put an end to this, it may happen all over again a hundred and fifty years from now."

"I knew things were going just a little too well. I'm in."

"What about Colin?"

"I'll let him decide, but once he finds out what's going down there is no way we can keep him out of this."

"Like uncle, like nephew."

Skye smiled.

"I also need to talk to Sean's dad."

"Sean's dad?"

"Yeah. I need to locate the witch's gravesite. I know it's on a small hill near the village that is bordered by two large stones, but I want to know where her grave is in case I need to move to Plan B."

"What's Plan B?"

"You don't want to know, but it involves shovels."

"Sorry I asked."

"It's going to take me a while to gather up all the necessary supplies. We won't be able to move out until this evening. I hate the delay, but we don't dare go in again before we're ready."

"Let me know when you need me."

"Thanks, Skye. I knew I could count on you."

My next task was to locate Dan, Sean's dad. Luckily, he was in Verona, which was quite often not the case. Mr. Hilton was an archaeologist whose area of expertise was classical archaeology, which meant he was more likely to be found in Egypt or Greece than the U.S.

I called Sean on my cell. He agreed to meet me with his dad in the study as soon as possible.

It did not take them long to arrive, but even so I paced the floor. Another spirit could emerge from a photograph at any moment and murder yet another innocent. Now that I knew what needed to be done, there was no time to waste.

"What's this about?" Sean asked as they entered.

"I need to find a grave."

"What grave?" Dan asked.

"The grave of Sarah Thornberry, The Witch of Wolf Creek."

"Just peachy," Sean said.

"I know approximately where she is buried, but I need to know the exact location."

"How approximately?"

"Maybe an area thirty by thirty feet."

"That shouldn't take long then. We can use geophysics," Dan said.

"What's that?" I asked.

"Ground penetrating radar. It's used to locate structures and items underground without disturbing a site. It's often used in preliminary archaeological surveys. The radar shoots a signal into the earth, which bounces back and is observed on a monitor."

"Do you have that equipment?"

"I can get it."

"How fast?"

"Couple hours if it's urgent."

"It is."

"I can leave to get it right away."

"Great, but it will probably be four hours before we can depart."

"Then I'll have plenty of time."

"What's this about?" Sean asked as soon as his dad had left.

I brought him up to speed as I had Skye earlier.

"Great. So we're going on another lunatic adventure?"

"The best kind."

"What can I do?"

"Make a trip to the grocery for me."

"What do you need?"

"A couple hundred pounds of salt."

"Seriously?"

I nodded.

"Anything else?"

"Your camera and any old camera that doesn't require a battery."

"Why no battery?"

"Sometimes ghosts drain power supplies. It's a precaution."

"Ah, okay. I guess I'm off to the store."

I went to my room and began gathering my own supplies. It took what was left of the afternoon to prepare and to load up the hearse, as well as Dan's truck. I nabbed Colin as soon as he returned from wrestling practice.

It was after six by the time we met at the hearse. Sean's dad followed me in his truck to the abandoned drive that was as close as we could get to Wolf Creek. Once there, he unloaded the gator the gardeners used at Graymoor and loaded his equipment and some of the salt into the back. The rest of us loaded up backpacks.

"Damn this is heavy," Sean said, testing the weight of his.

"No complaining. Skye and Colin took the heaviest packs."

"Yeah, this is a job for real men," Skye said. Sean stuck out his tongue.

"Okay, we're going to head directly for the small hill where the witch is buried. The first thing we do is ring the hill top with salt."

"To keep the spirits out or the witch in?" Colin asked.

"Both. We'll remain within the ring if we can, but it will likely be necessary to move through the site of the village to attract the ghosts. I haven't dealt with a witch before, so I'm not sure what's going to happen. If things get ugly with Sarah, get out of the ring and leave her to me."

"Witches can't cross salt?" Sean said.

"Dead witches can't. They're spirits like all the rest. Keep your cameras handy and shoot anything that moves. Dan, keep pace with us so we can guard you."

Sean's dad nodded.

A breeze began to blow as we set out and I heard the distant rumble of thunder. I hoped it did not rain for rain could easily break a circle of salt.

It was nearly dark under the trees. If the leaves had not already fallen the darkness in the forest would have been nearly complete. I kept a lookout, but I didn't expect company until we reached the village.

I was glad our mission did not rely on secrecy for the gator was loud enough to warn the spirits of our approach.

Each of us was watchful as we grew ever nearer to the village. Soon enough we reached it. All was eerily quiet. There was no sound except for the gator and the wind in the grass. At least it was lighter in the clearing, but the darkness was deepening as evening turned into night.

We passed through the village without incident and I guided Dan to the hill. When we arrived at our destination I wasted no time in directing Skye, Colin, and Sean to create a ring of salt around the hilltop while Dan set up his equipment.

I was more at ease when the ring was finished, but still vigilant. I could not have picked better companions for this night, but even so none of them were as well versed on the supernatural as me. I needed to guard them even as they guarded me.

Dan began with his work while the rest of us kept watch. Nothing at all happened for a handful of minutes, but then a silvery-gray shimmer, not unlike rising fog formed below us in the one-time location of Wolf Creek.

"Wow," Colin said as the spectral village began to take shape. At first the cabins, homes, and fences were transparent, but then they took on a solidity that surprised even me.

"It looks real," Skye said.

"Maybe it is, but... they're here," I said.

I could feel most spirits approach, but as before it was if a switch had been flipped on. One moment there was no ghostly presence. The next they were everywhere.

"There are a lot more of them this time. My suspicions were correct. The dead have returned to Wolf Creek."

"I can't see them," Colin said.

"They are there and they're coming," I said.

I could see them, as I could always see the spirits of the dead.

"Now is when the fun begins," Skye said, holding his camera but keeping one hand on his sword.

"There are at least thirty," I warned. "Wait until they are close."

The first of the spirits reached the base of the small hill. Their eyes were upon us. I read only anger and hatred in their gaze. There would be no reasoning with these spirits. They were cursed for what their village had once done to an elderly woman who, although she was truly a witch, had done them no harm.

"I can feel them," Colin said. I looked in his direction. He had his eyes closed as if searching with his mind. "The nearest is *there*." He pointed.

"You're right," I said.

I did not stop to wonder at Colin's ability for he had shown signs of being in touch with the dead before. His pet cat, Specter, was in fact a ghost that only he and I could see.

"Now I can see them," Colin said. "They're everywhere."

I detected no fear in Colin's voice. He was young, but he was his uncle's nephew in every way.

"I can see them now too," Skye said.

"Me too," Sean said.

"Be ready," I warned. The spirits were now visible to all. They were about to attack.

The first ghosts of Wolf Creek rushed forth, but even before they could reach the barrier of salt they disappeared in a blinding fury of electronic and mechanical clicks as we shot them with our cameras. We used no flashes for they were unnecessary and might frighten the spirits away.

"I guess that proves that theory," I said.

"So we captured their souls?" Colin asked.

"Some part of them, yes," I said.

More spirits came, but by no means all. Only those nearest took note of us. Sooner or later we would have to venture into the village.

"Got it," Dan said.

I hurried to see the outline on the monitor. It didn't look like much to me.

"Are you sure?"

"Yes, that is the only spot on the hill that has been disturbed in the last few hundred years. It's the right size for a grave. The readings are weak. There isn't much there, but that is the gravesite," Dan said, pointing to the monitor.

"Show me the location on the hill," I said.

Dan walked only a short distance and pointed out four small flags he had stuck in the ground.

"Right there."

"Guys. He found it. Start digging," I said.

"So we get to do all the physical labor," Skye said.

"I'm management. Besides, someone has to watch your back."

Everyone but me grabbed a shovel. I cast a glance over my shoulder. Three spirits were coming our way, but the ring of salt would hold them back. Digging up the witch was more important. She was the key.

I had reservations about what I had to do, but then my actions would ultimately force Sarah Thornberry into the next world. Some called it Heaven, but I knew there was no such place as most understood it; just as there was no Hell. She would be content there and free from the pain and hatred that I believed had likely driven her mad.

The guys made quick progress. Skye and Colin were both exceedingly strong and all knew just how important it was to get this done quickly. I was sure Dan was uneasy about plunging a shovel into what he likely viewed as an archaeological site, but we weren't here to study the burial. We were here to destroy it.

"Dig fast," I said as I sensed something I had not sensed before. It was like the sensation I felt at the coming of a spirit and yet unlike. I didn't like it. Something powerful and malevolent was coming through.

"I see bone," Dan said.

"Clear the earth away, quickly."

The guys worked as fast as possible, but we were out of time.

"Get out of the circle. Now!" I shouted.

Skye, Colin, Sean, and Dan didn't waste a second arguing. They bolted out of the circle so quickly Skye didn't even take the time to grab his camera. I saw him draw his sword even as the others wielded their cameras as if they were weapons.

A bright light like one might expect at the coming of an angel appeared, but what was coming was no angel. It was only a tiny point of light at first, but it grew and surrounding it was inky darkness that blotted out the few stars that had been visible between the clouds. The witch was coming.

I stood ready. I held up my hand and focused my thoughts even as Sarah Thornberry burst through and hovered some half-dozen feet above her grave. Her cloak and dress flowed about her and she cackled like a Halloween witch.

"Holy shit," Colin said.

"They are coming," warned Skye.

I didn't bother to turn. I left the spirits to the others.

"Sarah Thornberry, stay!" I shouted focusing the power of my mind upon her. I felt her push back, but I held her. "Those who wronged you are all dead. Now it is time for you to move on."

I pushed against her, but she was strong and I feared not entirely sane. I knew already I could not reason with her. She would not depart willingly. I took a deep breath and pushed against her with greater force. I began to tremble as she cackled loudly. She was too strong.

"Skye! Now!" I shouted, then shoved everything I had at the witch.

Skye knew what to do. I had feared we would come to this pass and we were prepared.

Skye fearlessly jumped into the circle, grabbed the gas can, and dumped it in the grave. Sarah knew her peril and attacked me. I trembled so violently with the effort I was putting forth I almost couldn't see. I felt my nose begin to bleed and my consciousness slip away, but I fought to remain awake.

"Hasta La Vista, Witch."

There was a flash of flame and heat and a scream. My last thought before I blacked out and fell to the ground was, *Did Skye really just say that?*

I was awakened by rain on my face. I slowly opened my eyes. I was so exhausted it was an effort.

"Marshall, are you okay?" Skye asked.

I focused on him as his features slowly changed from hazy and indistinct to sharp and clear.

"Hasta La Vista, Witch? Seriously?" I asked.

Skye shrugged. "I was caught up in the moment."

"The spirits?" I asked.

"All those who remained vanished when Skye lit the grave," Dan said.

"Are the cameras in the box?" I asked, trying to focus my thoughts, which felt like swimming upstream against a strong current.

"Just as you instructed."

"Oh my head hurts," I said.

I tried to rise up, but I couldn't. Skye lifted me and placed me in the passenger seat of the gator. I must have blacked out again, because the next time I opened my eyes I was in my own bed and it was morning.

"Talk about lazy," Skye said, putting his laptop aside. "We thought you'd never wake up."

"What time is it?"

"10 a.m."

"I did sleep in. I was exhausted."

"I'll say. It's 10 a.m. Saturday."

"What? Wait. I've been out for three days?"

"Yeah, we've taken turns watching over you. I don't ever want to hear you call me a laze ass again."

"Shit."

"Think you can stand?"

I sat up, then swung my legs over the side of the bed. I carefully stood.

"Yeah, I'm good."

"Go take a shower then. You stink. Then we'll get you something to eat."

"Yes, mother."

The shower awakened me, but I still wasn't fully awake as Skye led me downstairs to a small dining room. He must have alerted Martha I was coming because she had French toast, bacon, and eggs benedict waiting on me as well as hot English breakfast tea.

"Before you ask, the box is safe in my room."

"Good, although since we accomplished our goal I don't think it matters."

"You don't think the ghosts were captured in the photographs?"

"Oh, they were without a doubt, but when you destroyed the witch's remains and her spirit was forced into the next realm I believe the power of her curse was lifted. Those spirits will no longer be murderous, but just in case I will send them on. All the other spirits in the village departed the moment they had the chance so I don't think we have anything to worry about."

"Great. There are way too many old photographs in this house. Have you noticed? I don't like the idea that a spirit could pop out of one at any time and try to kill me."

"Oh, come on, Skye. That's a perfect excuse for you to wear your sword, although I doubt there will be any danger from other photos."

"You never know. Oh, I told the guys not to say anything."

"About what?"

"About you getting your ass kicked by a girl."

"She was a witch and she didn't kick my ass, but uh... thanks for the assist."

"That's what I'm here for, to save the world on a regular basis. It's a tough job, but no one else can do it."

"Uh huh."

I felt much better after breakfast. Once I finished, Skye and I headed up to his room to retrieve the box that had the ability to trap spirits due to the layer of salt trapped between two layers of wood on all sides. We took the box to my room and poured a circle of salt around it. I opened the box, pulled out a camera, and placed it on the table within the ring of salt. I didn't anticipate trouble, but I wanted to keep things manageable just in case.

I performed a standard exorcism to the next world, but nothing happened.

"That was anticlimactic," Skye said.

"Which is very good news. That means the spirits departed when the witch's remains were destroyed."

I pulled out the rest of the cameras and repeated the exorcism on all of them at once to make certain. Again, nothing happened.

"We have succeeded," I said.

"It's a good thing this isn't a movie. This would be a lame ass ending."

"Well, this isn't a movie, nor is it the end. You know a new problem will crop up soon."

"With that thought in mind, I'm going to have a swim before the zombie apocalypse or whatever is next begins."

"Have fun. I might take a nap."

"Seriously? Wow, you are lazy."

"Shut up, Skye."

Skye grinned and departed.

I did take a nap. I slept for a few more hours and awakened in time for supper. Skye clapped for me as I entered the dining room.

"I think I'm rested up now," I said.

"I would hope so."

After a supper of fried chicken, mashed potatoes with cream gravy, corn, and a hot yeast roll with real butter I was not only rested, but full. Even so, I managed to eat a piece of pecan pie.

Sean, Skye, Colin, Dan and I gathered in a nearby parlor after supper to discuss the events of a few nights before.

"Skye said we succeeded," Dan said.

"We did. Thank you all. I couldn't have done it alone."

Skye cleared his throat.

"Coming down with something, Skye?" I asked.

Skye glared at me, but then grinned.

"So it would be safe to go back out there? I'd like another look at the ghost village," Colin said.

"It will be safe, but I'm not sure the village will reappear. It seemed to be connected to the spirits who resided there."

"That blows."

"I could be wrong."

"I'm planning on leading an excavation there," Dan said. "I've been talking to George at the historical society and he thought it would be a great program for anyone interested in local history or archaeology. He also wants to work with the high school. It can be a learning experience for students and the community and we can discover a lot about Wolf Creek at the same time."

"That sounds great," I said. Dan was clearly enthused by the idea.

"George has already talked with the land owner. He's very much in favor of the idea. We may begin as early as next spring."

"Are you sure you'll be around then?" Sean asked since his dad was away as often as not.

"I'm going to take it on as a project. I'll be here."

"Oh, I called Thad and told him about our most recent adventures. He wants to do a book on it," Skye said.

"I think the main character should be Marshall: The Witch Hunter," I said.

"No way! It will be all about me! Skye Mackenzie: The Witch Slayer."

"Uh huh."

We reminisced about our adventure and then went our separate ways. When I returned to my room I pulled out the journal of Theodorus Blackwood. I needed to return it to the historical society as soon as possible since I was sure George would want to thoroughly research it. What had been a neglected relic was now a key artifact of Verona's history.

I read the journal in its entirety. Theodorus Blackwood lived to be an old man. He moved the short distance from Wolf Creek to Verona after he completed his task there. Having recently completed my own task in the same village, I turned back to the last entry he wrote at Wolf Creek.

"I leave tomorrow and with me the one-time village of Wolf Creek will expire. What was once a thriving village has now been reduced to a population of one. I have remained all this time to make certain that no ghosts remain to trouble the living and at last I am certain that nothing remains here except abandoned homes, hopes, graves, and dreams.

"In time, no one will believe what I have written in this journal, but it matters not. I'll know what happened was real and so will those who survived. I am eager to put this place behind me and look forward to my prospects in Verona, where I will soon open my own photography studio. May Wolf Creek now rest in peace along with those buried here."

Theodorus was wrong. He would be remembered because the ghosts of the past had returned once more. Now, more than a hundred and fifty years later the story had finally ended—or at least so I hoped.

Gods of The Old Forest

Verona, Indiana
June 2008

"The ghosts aren't attacking you. They're trying to communicate," I said.

"Communicate? They tried to suffocate me!"

My cell phone rang. I glanced at the number.

"I should take this," I said, then answered. "What can I do for you sheriff? Yes, I read about it in *The Citizen*. Another one? Okay, I can be there in half an hour. Bye."

"I'm sorry about that. The spirits weren't actually trying to suffocate you. I'm sure the experience was terrifying, but you weren't in physical danger."

"They nearly scared me to death! How is suffocating me communicating?"

"That's how they died."

"How do you know that?"

"I could feel it and I spoke to one of them. There is an old mine beneath your home. It was part of a tunnel that ran under most of the homes on this street. In the 1890's there was a tunnel collapse. Eight men were buried alive. No attempt was made to rescue them because it was believed they were killed instantly. They weren't."

My customer gazed at me with shock and compassion in her eyes.

"They were trapped in a small area for two days, waiting and hoping for rescue as they slowly began to run out of air. Then the earth above them gave way and suffocated them to death. What you felt is what they felt. They just want someone to know what happened to them. They want to be remembered. I promised them that I would go to Mr. Madison, the director of the Verona Historical Society Museum and tell him their story so it can be written down and remembered. I'll keep my promise to them. You won't have any more problems with them. I convinced them it was time to go on."

"So they really weren't trying to hurt me? They only wanted me to know what happened to them? That's so sad. What a horrible way to die."

"Don't worry. They will be fine now and so will you."

"I can't thank you enough, Marshall."

"You're welcome. I'm glad to help. I should get going. The sheriff wants my help on a case."

"The murder in The Old Forest?"

"Murders. There has been another."

Mrs. Gottenmyer wrote me a check and thanked me again. I walked out to my hearse and drove out of town, past the old Chamberlain house, and on a bit further to the edge of The Old Forest.

The woods had been called that for time out of mind and for good reason. The forest was old, unthinkably old. It was perhaps the last bit of forest left of the great forest that once covered most of the Midwest. Many of the trees were almost impossibly huge. There were oaks in the wood with trunks so thick that six grown men could not reach all the way around. The forest had been undisturbed for centuries, but that had recently changed.

I spotted the sheriff's car parked near a mobile office like those used on construction sites. Just beyond were members of Eco Force holding signs protesting the imminent destruction of a large section of the forest. Further beyond was a section cordoned off by yellow police tape.

I spotted the sheriff and walked out to meet him. The protestors didn't bother me, likely because at least a couple of them recognized me and knew I was not associated with Lewdcorp, the development group that intended to destroy the forest.

"Marshall, I'm glad you could come," the sheriff said when he spotted me.

"I must admit I'm at a loss as to why you asked me, Allen. You know I deal with the supernatural. Unless you think there is something paranormal going on here."

"To tell you the truth, I don't know what's going on. We have two unexplained murders. The first was five days ago. We found a victim at the edge of the woods who was strangled to death. The thing is, the ground was wet and the only footprints were those of the victim and of the man who discovered the body. The footprints were quite clear. The area was muddy and I don't see how the murderer could have failed to leave footprints."

"Perhaps the man who says he discovered the body is the murderer."

The sheriff shook his head. "No, we thought of that, but his prints stop a good twelve feet away. Anyway, the second murder is even more bizarre. I'd like you to take a look, but I warn you it's a gruesome sight."

"I'm accustomed to gruesome."

"Then follow me."

Allen led me into the forest. Soon, trees surrounded us. I felt a sense of watchfulness, as if the forest itself was observing us. The Old Forest was a queer place. There were lots of stories and rumors about it. Strange creatures were said to dwell there and many in and around Verona would not step foot inside for any amount of money. Others visited to hike, hunt mushrooms, or enjoy one of the most incredible stands of old-growth oaks, tulip trees, maples, elms, and sycamores in the U.S. It was a true shame it was about to be destroyed. My sympathies were with the protestors.

"Brace yourself," the sheriff said as we rounded an enormous oak.

I turned my attention from the trees to the ground, but there was no body in sight.

"Uh..." I began, but then the sheriff pointed up. I gazed upward. A man wearing a fluorescent vest hung from a vine. His feet were a good fifteen feet above the forest floor. His body was as many feet out from the trunk of the tree.

"How do you explain that?" the sheriff asked.

"Suicide, but if so how did he climb the tree?" The lowest limbs were above the corpse. There was no way anyone could have climbed up without a ladder or some type of climbing rig.

"We thought of that, but there is no sign of climbing tackle or damage to the trunk of the tree from spikes."

I whistled. "This is a puzzle."

Firemen arrived with a long ladder and other equipment. Soon, the coroner arrived. I walked around the area, examining the ground and the surrounding trees. I could feel something here, but it wasn't ghosts. I had the ability to see ghosts and none were present. What I felt was unusual and yet somehow familiar. Whatever it was felt "distant," as if it was in another part of the forest. I had no idea if what I sensed had any connection to the dead man hanging from the tree. The Old Forest was indeed a queer place with many secrets. I loved it here.

It took quite a while to get the body down. I stepped in for a closer look as the police photographer and coroner began their work.

"I've never seen anything like this," the coroner said, pointing to the thick vine around the victim's neck. "It looks as if it grew around his neck. I don't see how else it could have gotten there, but how is that possible?"

The sheriff looked at me.

"I've never seen anything like this either, but it looks as if the vine is the murderer," I said.

"Like I'm going to put that in a report," the sheriff said.

I took some photos of my own and made a few notes as the coroner worked to cut away the vine.

"How does this compare with the previous murder?" I asked when he'd finished and could see the bruising and abrasions on the neck.

"Very similar. The first victim had nothing around his neck, but these marks are much the same. A vine could easily have been used to kill the first victim."

"What do you think, Marshall?"

"I've got nothing right now except a vague sense of a presence in the forest. I don't know if it has anything to do with the murders. I'll do some research and check into the history of this place. That may give me some ideas. I'll let you know."

"Thanks, Marshall."

"Hey, thanks for asking me. The supernatural may well be at work here. In fact, at this point I don't see how it couldn't be."

I returned to the hearse and drove back into town. I parked near the Verona Historical Society Museum and walked inside. George Madison, the director, greeted me.

"What brings you in, Marshall?"

"Two things actually—a message from the grave and a murder."

"I'll say one thing for you—you're never boring. Let's go in the back."

George led me to his office, where we both sat down. First, I explained my recently finished case and gave him the information provided by the spirit of the dead miner. Most historians would have scoffed, but George was too well acquainted with the supernatural and with my abilities to doubt.

"The miners want to be remembered. They want their story to be known."

"We're in the business of remembering here. I'll take care of it," George said as he finished taking notes. "Now, on to the murder."

"There has been another murder in The Old Forest, a rather unexplainable one."

"Another? When?"

"Very recently. I came directly here from the crime scene. What can you tell me about the forest?"

"Fact or myth and legend?"

"Let's begin with fact."

"It's likely the last untouched forest in the state. There are numerous trees there well over two hundred years old and some far older. It's a great example of what the forests were like when the first Native Americans moved into the region."

"The Native Americans, not the European settlers?"

"Yes. The various Native American groups who lived in the area changed the landscape little compared to the early settlers and those who came after, but they did change it and used considerable amounts of wood. When the settlers began to arrive the landscape had already changed."

"Why is The Old Forest unchanged then?"

"That's an interesting question. The Native Americans considered it a sacred place. It was a place were spirits dwelled. There were a number of different Native American groups who lived in the area over the last several centuries, but this belief seems to have been held in common. Entering the forest, gathering berries, nuts, and whatever else the land offered was acceptable, but harming the forest or anything in it was forbidden."

"Why did the settlers leave it alone?"

"Many of the early settlers picked up the beliefs of the Native Americans. Tragedy befell those who did not respect The Old

Forest. There are very early accounts of men being killed by trees they chopped down in the forest and other accidents claiming the lives of those who harmed the forest."

"When you say the trees killed them—what do you mean?"

"I mean that when the tree being cut down fell, it fell on the man wielding the axe. It happened so frequently that The Old Forest soon gained the same reputation with the settlers as it had with those who came before. You have to remember that men then were experts at felling trees. Many cut down hundreds or even thousands in their lifetime. They knew what they were doing and an accident such as having a tree fall on them was rare, except in the Old Forest."

"Was there any mention of trees killing men in other ways?"

"Nothing specific, but here is where we cross into myth and legend. The early settlers came to believe that the forest protected itself. They believed the forest itself would retaliate if harmed. I've never run across any specifics, but the settlers soon began to avoid the forest and considered it a cursed place."

"What has preserved the forest in more modern times?" I asked.

"Tradition, partly. There are some who yet today consider it a cursed location and there have been a number of deaths in the forest over the past decades. Many merely consider it a dangerous place to be avoided. I can't really explain how the forest has managed to remain untouched, but it does seem its luck has run out. It's a shame that a large part of it is slated to be cut down."

"I wouldn't be so sure about that. Both of the murder victims were employees of Lewdcorp, the development group who bought a section of the forest and intends to destroy it for their project."

"Interesting. I've heard that the protestors are the main suspects."

"An idea no doubt pushed by Lewdcorp. They are the most obvious suspects, but the obvious are rarely guilty. I'm quite certain that they are innocent of the latest murder."

"Why?"

"Because the victim was killed by a vine. What's more he was killed by a vine growing around his neck."

"That's rather hard to believe."

"Yes it is, especially considering that vines grow very slowly, but I viewed the body after it was taken down. The vines weren't merely wrapped around the neck, they looked as if they had grown around the victim's neck."

"It sounds like something right up your alley."

"I don't believe there are ghosts involved, but there is a presence in the forest. I have no idea what it is or if it's connected to the murders, but I think the Native Americans had reason to believe as they did. Now, what can you tell me about the myths and legends connected to The Old Forest?"

"Most of it is vague. The Native Americans believed it was inhabited by strange beasts and beings, although none that were considered dangerous, merely unknown outside the forest. It was the settlers who first mentioned dangerous creatures, some real, some mythical. There is little doubt that the accounts of bears, panthers, and wolves residing in the woods are real, but there are also tales of flying lizards, witches, wild boys, and unnamed hairy creatures of enormous size. Most of it has come down as folklore, but there are a few newspaper accounts of encounters."

"I didn't realize The Old Forest was this interesting," I said.

"Most places are interesting if you know their history. The Old Forest has always had a strange reputation. The number of disappearances there alone is of note."

"How many?"

"Since the 1830s around two dozen."

"That's a lot, even for that long of a time span. Do you know if any of those lost were found, either dead or alive?"

"Few who were lost in The Old Forest were ever seen again. The bodies of three or four were discovered and about the same number of children who were lost inside made their way back out again. Strangely, and I'm sure you'll like this; the children mentioned being guided out by a boy. What's most interesting is that even though the accounts given by the children are separated by decades, they describe the same boy."

"That is interesting. Can I get copies of the newspapers that have these accounts and those that mention other disappearances?"

"Yes, you can. The Old Forest is one of my many projects. I've assembled quite a bit of resource material over the years and

169

the volunteers inform me anytime they find something in the archives, which you know we're still cataloging. I can probably have copies for you by tomorrow at the latest. It will take some time to pull everything out and copy it."

"Great. Thank you so much, George."

We talked more, then I headed back to the hearse and Graymoor Mansion.

As I walked through the mansion I thought about the murders, what George had told me, and the presence I'd felt in the forest. This wasn't at all like most of my cases that involved hauntings, angry spirits, or other supernatural phenomena, but there was something strange going on and that was enough for me.

I had not paid much attention to where I was going and found myself in The Solarium, which was an enormous room made almost entirely of glass. I breathed in the scent of living things as I walked along one of the many paths. The afternoon sun made the vast greenhouse bright, revealing the plants in all their glory. The air was warm and humid and oxygen rich. Depending on the path one chose one might see roses or bamboo or lemon and orange trees or woodland flowers. There were stone benches to sit upon and take in the surrounding natural beauty. Depending on where one sat, one could sit among citrus trees, a Japanese garden, or familiar daisies, coneflowers, and herbs. The Solarium was one of the most popular parts of the bed & breakfast and yet it was nearly always quiet and peaceful. I could feel alone here even when several others were wandering the garden.

I liked to come here to think and sometimes merely to breathe. The scent of flowering plants and herbs filled the air. The sound of the resident birds chirping and the fountain flowing further added to the atmosphere. It was especially nice to visit in winter and see green, thriving plants while all was cold and bleak outside, but even during a sunny day in June it was enjoyable.

I kept pondering the mystery of The Old Forest as I walked through the gardens and then through the hallways of Graymoor Mansion. I passed works of art, antique vases, and even a suit of armor. Living in Graymoor was like living in a museum.

I wandered into the Natatorium where Skye was just climbing out of the pool. Water cascaded down over his muscular defined body. I noticed a couple of older women and two high school boys checking him out.

"I see you're being a slacker again," I said.

"I just finished giving a swimming lesson. I notice you're not doing anything."

"I'm working. I'm thinking about my newest case."

"You call thinking working? Ha. What's this case about? No. Don't tell me. Zombie attacks? Statues coming to life? A witchdoctor?"

"No. A forest."

"Wow. I am disappointed." Sky quipped.

"Disappointed in what?" Colin asked as he walked toward us from the locker room. Colin was Skye's nephew and looked like a seventeen-year-old version of his twenty-seven-year-old uncle.

"Marshall. He's taken up gardening instead of hunting ghosts."

"I have not. This case involves The Old Forest and murders."

"Don't you mean murder?" Skye asked.

"No. Murders. There has been another and it looks like the forest itself committed this one. In fact, it may possibly have committed the first one as well."

"Okay, that is a little interesting, but not as interesting as a zombie attack."

"I have to agree," Colin said.

Colin left us and dove into the pool.

"I'd like you to come with me to The Old Forest sometime in the next few days and get your impression."

"I think you just want me to be your bodyguard."

"While that is a plus, I don't think I'll need one. The Old Forest doesn't appear to be dangerous, except to those who wish it harm."

"Okay, I'll make a note not to bring an axe. What do you think is going on there?"

"I'm not at all sure yet. George is sending me some information on disappearances and other strange occurrences in the forest. I hope to find a pattern or something that matches what's happening now."

"Oh, research. That is boring. Contact me when you get to the exciting stuff."

"You sure you don't want to join me later, Skye? We can read old newspapers and journal entries and take notes."

"That would be a huge NO."

I laughed.

"Good luck, although I don't you think need it. You haven't failed to solve a case yet," Skye said.

"Oh! A compliment! How rare!"

"Yeah, don't get used to it. Now, some of us have real work to do. See you later, Marshall."

"Bye."

I smiled and shook my head as I left the Natatorium. Skye would never change, at least I hoped not.

I followed the twisting hallways of the mansion back toward the lobby. It was one of the many routes I had memorized so there was no danger of getting lost.

"Marshall, I was about to call you. This just arrived for you," Sean said as I walked into the main lobby.

"Great, I've been waiting for that. I'm working on a new case involving the murders in The Old Forest."

"Murders?"

For what felt like the tenth time I explained that a second murder had been committed in the forest. I then gave Sean a quick overview of the details.

"I'm glad I don't have to try to figure it out. I think running a hotel is far easier. Let me know if you need my help."

"Will do," I said as I took the box and began the long trek upstairs to my room. Sean, Skye, Colin, and even Sean's dad had helped me on previous cases. I could always count on my friends.

When I reached my room I placed the box on a large marble-topped Victorian desk that sat near the window. The box was filled with files and photocopies. I had a long evening and likely night ahead, but I couldn't wait to get started. As Sherlock Holmes said, "The game was afoot."

***

"You might want to read this," Skye said, handing me the local paper as we sat in the dining room eating breakfast. I put aside my eggs benedict and French toast with blueberries for a moment to check it out.

The Verona Citizen –
Tuesday, June 10, 2008:

LEWDCORP & ECOFORCE BATTLE OVER THE OLD FOREST ESCALATES

The environmental protest group, Ecoforce, and development group Lewdcorp have been at odds over the proposed construction of a planned retail/residential complex for several months now. The ensuing court battle delayed the project for months, but the last legal hurtle was navigated by Lewdcorp two weeks ago and bulldozers are now poised to begin clearing a section of what is known as The Old Forest. The legal battle is over, but Ecoforce is not giving up the fight.

"Destroying 30% of pristine old-growth forest is an ecological crime," Noah Gresham of Ecoforce stated. "The local community has been against this project from the beginning, but Lewdcorp is determined to press ahead so the company can make a buck. That is Lewdcorp's one and only concern—profit."

"The courts have ruled in our favor," stated Lewdcorp spokesman, Jeff Graham. "We have a right to do with this property as we see fit. Our project will provide jobs and benefit the local community, but Ecoforce continues to harass our workers and stir up trouble. Two employees of Lewdcorp have been murdered in the course of a week. One does not have to look far to find suspects."

Local and state law enforcement are currently investigating The Old Forest murders, but so far have come up with no strong suspects. Several persons of interest have been questioned, but authorities are at a loss as to who might have committed the crimes or even how they were committed.

"These are the most unusual murders we have ever investigated," said Sheriff Griffith. "On the surface, the circumstances in which they were committed seem impossible and yet two men have died. We've brought in outside help, but currently everyone is baffled. We intend to get to the bottom of this, but it will take time."

Ecoforce continues to picket and signatures on petitions against construction have now passed the 100,000 mark, but Lewdcorp has scheduled site preparation to begin next week.

"This project is going forward. It will happen," Graham stated. "No one wants this project except Lewdcorp," stated Gresham. "We will do everything we can within the law to protect this forest."

The battle over The Old Forest continues and neither side is willing to give in. What will be the outcome? We can but wait and see.

"These Lewdcorp guys are assholes," I said.

Skye laughed. "I agree."

"Are any of them staying in the mansion?"

"I told them we are booked solid for the next several months. They are not welcome here," Sean said.

"How is your ultra-boring research coming?" Skye asked.

"It's fascinating, and I'd bet money that Lewdcorp is going to lose their battle. The forest, or something within it, has a history of protecting it. There is a reason those trees have remained untouched. Anyone who tries to harm them pays the price."

"Wasn't the last guy murdered only a surveyor?" Sean asked.

"Yes, in the employ of Lewdcorp. He was surveying for the initial site preparation. He was viewed as a danger and he died for it."

"You don't think these Ecoforce people have anything to do with the murders?" Skye asked.

"No. I talked to the sheriff. He's checked on them. They are non-violent. They've protested environment destruction all over the country. They often put themselves in harm's way, but they have never harmed anyone. It would be a violation of their basic philosophy."

"There are a lot of other people pissed off about this project. A lot of locals are joining the protest," Sean said.

"True, but the fact is that the murders were committed by supernatural means. I am absolutely certain of it now," I said, turning to Skye. "Want to go on a field trip?"

"I thought you'd never ask."

"Just don't bring your sword. You do not want the forest to get the wrong idea."

"No sword? Where's the fun in that?"

**

"You ready?" I asked Skye as I met him at the bottom of the stairs.

"I'm always ready, but I'm driving."

"What? You don't want to ride in my fine automobile?"

"I've ridden in your hearse enough. It's a perfect day to drive the Auburn."

Skye owned a 1935 Auburn boattail speedster. It was a truly beautiful car and Skye's prized possession. It should have been. It cost more than most houses.

"Who is watching the Natatorium and the gym?"

"I bribed Colin into taking over for me. It didn't take much. He's there much of the time anyway."

"Yeah, you and your nephew have that sick working-out obsession."

"It's not an obsession. It's a lifestyle."

"It's too much work, is what it is," I said as we walked to the old carriage house where our cars were stored.

"Not if you enjoy it."

"Which I don't."

I opened the door. Skye went inside, started up his Auburn, and slowly pulled it out. It was a beautiful car with sleek lines. The rear tapered to a point so that it looked like the prow of a boat.

"You'd think there would be more room, considering what you paid for this thing," I said after I closed the garage door and climbed into the single seat.

"There is plenty of room for two."

"Perhaps, but no more."

"Not many people are cool enough to ride in this car."

"I made the cut."

"Well, I like you so I bent the rules for you."

"You are so gracious."

Skye drove out of town toward The Old Forest. We soon arrived. Protestors holding signs stood near the forest. Bulldozers and other large equipment was parked in a makeshift lot.

"I'm surprised Lewdcorp doesn't have them arrested for trespassing," Skye said, looking at the protestors.

"They can't. They are standing on land that doesn't belong to Lewdcorp. The owner is among them."

"Is he the guy who sold part of the forest to the developers?"

"No. That's the edge of his farm. It meets The Old Forest on the east side."

"Will the protestors give us trouble?" Skye asked.

"No. They know I'm here investigating and that I'm on their side. You'll recognize some of them as we pass near."

Skye and I traveled light. We carried only small backpacks that contained water bottles, food, and a few other things we might possibly need.

I didn't think we were in any danger, but having Skye by my side set me at ease. He could handle anything.

We stepped into the forest and were quickly concealed by the trees. The oaks, sycamores, and other trees were enormous even near the borders. Ferns, moss, and other plants flourished everywhere.

"This is a beautiful place. I've never been very deep inside. I've always wanted to explore," Skye said.

"Today is your chance."

The canopy cut off most of the sunlight and yet the forest floor was illuminated with green light filtering through the leaves. The air smelled even cleaner and richer than that in the Solarium.

"So where are we going? Do you have a destination in mind?" Skye asked.

"I feel a presence in the forest. We are going wherever it is. It's possible the forest itself is aware and protecting itself, but I have a feeling that it isn't the forest. It's whatever I feel inside it. Do you feel anything?"

"I feel as if I do, but I don't know if I'm actually feeling it or if I just think I am because you said there is a presence. Then again, I don't sense ghosts at all so maybe I am."

We continued moving forward. Grape and other vines trailed down from the trees here and there. I remembered the man choked to death by vines, but I wasn't afraid. We were not here to harm the trees or anything else.

"This reminds me a bit of Tydannon. I'd love to find some grapes like those that grow there."

"I'd rather find some chocolate," I said. In Tydannon, chocolate, real chocolate and not merely cocoa beans, actually grew on bushes.

The deeper we walked into the forest, the larger it seemed. The Old Forest was quite large, but by no means vast. I had driven around its borders on country roads so I had a good idea of its extent, but even so it seemed larger than it should have been. Perhaps it was my lack of familiarity with the woods, but it was also possible that it was larger than it appeared. Graymoor Mansion was like that. While the mansion was enormous, its outside dimensions could not account for all the rooms and space inside. I knew. I'd measured.

"I should walk out here just to breathe," Skye said. "The air in Verona is fairly clean, but this air is so pure."

"Thanks to the trees and plants. We need more of them, not less."

"That development project has to be stopped," Skye said.

"I don't think you need to be concerned. I have a feeling it's not going to happen."

We passed crystal clear streams as we walked. Here and there were small clearings and in these spaces were grassy meadows where wild, sun-loving plants dwelled. In one meadow was a profusion of black-eye Susans, which were native to Indiana. Mostly, there were trees the like of which was not often seen in our time. I had seen trees like this only once before…

"We're getting very close," I said.

"Yes, we are," Skye said, grinning.

I turned to see what he was looking at. My breath caught in my throat for a moment. I recognized the boy who stood near gazing at us with merry mischief in his eyes. I had met this boy or others like him before, but he could not possibly be here.

"Hello, Skye. Hello, Marshall. Welcome to The Forest. Follow me, Pan is waiting."

I looked toward Skye with my eyes wide with wonder.

"How is this possible?" I asked.

"Does it matter?" Skye said.

The boy took us each by the hand and pulled us yet deeper into the forest. I gazed at the boy as we walked hand-in-hand. He was clad only with a loincloth and a vine angled over his torso and another encircling his brow. He looked to be about twelve or thirteen, but I knew he was older, far, far older. He was one of Pan's wild boys; the same mentioned in ancient Greek myths, and even then he was already unthinkably old.

My mind raced as we walked between the enormous trunks of the trees. Skye and I had met the wild boys and Pan himself in a forest before, but it was in a place far, far away—a world once connected to this one, but now sundered.

I knew we were growing close when I began to notice wild grape vines in ever-greater profusion. I would have known in any case because I could feel the presence of Pan. I could sense all spirits, but they were as a candle to a star when compared with Pan. He was, after all, an actual god.

We soon entered what looked like a great hall with walls of enormous oaks and grape vines, a roof of interlaced limbs and more vines, and a carpet of lush, green grass with purple crocus creating a pattern. The hall was filled with a green light. A dozen or more wild boys danced around us, greeting and patting us as if welcoming back old friends. At the end of the hall, standing and gazing at us was the god Pan.

Pan appeared to be a youth of astounding beauty, but like the wild boys he was old beyond reckoning. Most nowadays would claim he was nothing but a myth, but he had been worshipped once upon a time, and he was undeniably real. What he was, I did not know. He was powerful, dangerous without question, and unpredictable. I believe it was Skye who once said he looked like a boy who might do *anything*. He possessed enormous dominance over all growing things. I was quite sure he could be terrifying, but we had found him friendly, especially Skye.

"It is good to see you again," Pan said as we drew near.

"It is even better to see you," I said and meant it. With Pan present I knew The Old Forest was in no danger.

"Yet you wonder how it is possible," Pan said.

"Yes."

"It is not easy for most to pass from one world to another, but I am not most. I do not come here often, but I come when I am needed."

"I knew the forest was retaliating against those who tried to harm it. Now, I understand how," I said.

"There are places in your world that are protected and they will forever remain so. Have no fear for this forest. Concern yourself with it not at all. Instead, let us celebrate our meeting."

At that, food and wine appeared on living tables of grape vines. There were strawberries of enormous size such as I had not seen since we departed from Tydannon. There were blueberries the size of plums and plums the size of grapefruit. There was, in fact, every fruit that one could possibly name and some one could not.

I bowed my head slightly and stepped toward the table where the wild boys were already eating. As I did so, Pan stepped toward Skye and grasped his hands. I turned away so I did not see what transpired between them. Pan and Skye had a special relationship that I felt was their own, and not to be observed by me.

I took one of the gold cups decorated with figures of wild boys dancing and took a sip. I had drunk Pan's wine before and knew it was beyond potent. A single cup was enough to make me drunk, so I went very easy on it and focused my attention on the fruit instead.

When I looked back toward Skye, he had disappeared and so had Pan. I was not in the least worried. While Pan had the power to do anything to either of us he wished, I knew he meant us no harm. I was powerfully curious about what Pan and Skye were up to, but it is not wise to interfere in the lives of gods.

I quickly lost track of time, for this was one of those places where time had no meaning or perhaps did not exist at all. Skye and Pan returned at some point, but exactly when I did not know. Later, I remembered only that we ate, drank, laughed, and danced. It was like that when one was with Pan.

I awakened the next morning on the grass. Pan and his wild boys were gone, but plenty of food and drink remained. Skye lay near me. He was awake and gazed up at the canopy of leaves and vines overhead with his arms behind his head.

"Did you finally decided to wake up?" he asked.

I sat up and shook my head. I took a deep breath.

"Let's have breakfast and then head back," I said.

Skye and I feasted on fruit leftover from the party, but did not have any wine. Instead, we drank only water. I gazed at Skye while I ate, wondering again what happened during the night. My memories were fuzzy, which came as no surprise at all.

Skye smiled at me as if he knew or could guess what I was thinking, but he said nothing.

"They're still in the forest, I can feel them," I said.

"Me too, but I do not think we will see them again, at least not for a long time."

I nodded and we headed back.

We took our time for the forest was indescribably beautiful and there was no urgency. The Old Forest was in absolutely no danger. It never had been and never would be in danger. No matter who claimed to own it or control it their claims were meaningless. No one held power over this forest, except for Pan.

When we emerged from the forest, the bulldozers and protestors were still there. Workmen had come and were even now climbing into the equipment and starting it up.

"What should we do? Warn them?" Skye asked.

"Do you think they would listen? We stand back and see what happens."

Even as I spoke, the wind got up and clouds darkened what had been a perfectly clear sky. The darkness deepened and thunder rumbled in warning. Rain began to pour from the sky, but only on the would-be destroyers. The protestors, Skye, and myself remained dry.

"It's truly not wise to anger a nature god," I said.

The first dozer moved forward. The thunder rumbled ominously and the earth began to tremble. For a moment, it looked as if several giant moles were tunneling beneath the earth, but then enormous roots erupted from the ground and enveloped the bulldozer. The operator was only just able to jump clear before the powerful piece of machinery was crushed and pulled beneath the earth.

No other equipment moved forward. Bolts of lightning lashed out at the machines. The workmen bolted and ran away as fast as they could manage. The roots finished off the machines, reaching out from below and rending the metal to shreds like some earth cousin of the Kraken of the deep sea. In moments, all had been pulled below the earth and there was no sign of the machinery, the construction office, or anything else connected with Lewdcorp. Grass sprouted in the churned up earth and grew even as we watched. In less than a minute, a meadow of grass and wildflowers stood before us.

The protestors gaped open-mouthed, but Skye and I smiled.

"I believe we're done here," I said. "On to the next case, unless you want to tell me what you and Pan got up to last night."

"Not on your life," Skye said.

Dr. Stupendous Smith's Carnival of Astonishment

Verona, Indiana
May 2008

"It's back," Colin said as I opened the door to my room in Graymoor Mansion.

"What's back? The McRib sandwich, bell-bottoms, what?"

"What are bell-bottoms?"

"Think of them as the opposite of skinny-jeans, but never mind. What's back?"

"The carnival."

"Let's go, then. We have no time to waste. Is Skye around?"

"I think so."

"Call him. I don't want to take any chances and we have to move fast. If we miss our opportunity, we'll have to wait another twenty-five years."

"You'll be dead by then," Colin said with a smirk.

"Shut it and call."

Colin laughed. He placed the call as we walked through the hallways of the mansion and down the stairs.

"He said he'll meet us in the lobby. He was in the Natatorium. So you think this might be dangerous?"

"This carnival has been coming to Verona once every twenty-five years for more than a century. Every time it does, people go missing. I call that dangerous."

Skye crossed the lobby as we reached the foot of the stairs. He was wearing khaki shorts and a tee-shirt that was too tight in the arms and chest. It wasn't that the shirt was too small, just that Skye's arms and chest were that muscular. Colin's polo was similarly stretched across his torso—like uncle, like nephew.

I gazed at Colin for a moment.

"What?" he asked.

"Are you getting taller or am I getting shorter?"

"You may be getting shorter. I think Skye is too. I've heard elderly guys like you shrink as you get older."

"We're both 27, Colin."

"Oh my God. That's practically dead! You better enjoy yourself while you can. You don't have much time left."

Skye grabbed Colin, put him in a headlock, and mussed his hair before releasing him.

"Not cool!" Colin said.

"You know, I'd smack you if weren't capable of kicking my ass with one arm tied behind your back," I said.

"Aww, I'd never hurt you, Marshall. You're far too cool."

"Well, that's true," I said. Colin laughed.

We walked across the lobby and out the front door.

"So, what's going on?" Skye asked as we crossed the lawn and left Graymoor Mansion behind us.

"The carnival is back and right on schedule."

"The one you told me about?"

"Yes. Dr. Stupendous Smith's Carnival of Astonishment."

"Is this going to be another long, drawn-out investigation with lots of boring research?"

"Like you've ever helped with the research part."

"Hey, these are your investigations. I only help you out of the goodness of my heart."

"Uh huh. Anyway, I've already done the research. That's how I discovered the pattern. Every time this carnival visits Verona, people disappear; kids and teens mainly. It happened in 1983, 1958, 1933, 1908, 1883, and perhaps even before, but there are no records of the carnival coming to town before 1883."

"If people go missing every time the carnival comes to town, why don't the cops do something about it?" Skye asked.

"It comes and goes with little notice. It's only advertising is flyers and word of mouth. I got interested in it after I read a 1933 journal that told of the carnival appearing in a meadow outside of town. It wasn't there one moment and was the next. The author of the journal thought she might be going crazy. She told no one."

"Maybe she *was* crazy," Colin said.

"Perhaps, but I doubt it. I've come across hints and bits and pieces of evidence that have convinced me this is no ordinary carnival. If it can appear in an instant, it could disappear just as quickly and I don't think we want to be there when it does."

The last light of the setting sun disappeared and the shadows deepened as we followed Colin. In the distance, I could hear calliope music that sounded both eerie and mournful. Soon, we could see the glow of lights in the distance and then the lights themselves.

The carnival was situated on the edge of town in a large field. Even from our location I could make out a Ferris wheel, a carousel, and the Midway. As we drew closer I could see people coming and going. The music grew louder, but was no less eerie to my ears.

Soon, we approached the entrance where a grimacing clown on high stilts juggled flaming torches. Behind him was an enormous banner reading, "Dr. Stupendous Smith's Carnival of Astonishment."

We walked beneath the banner under the watchful eyes of the clown, and entered the carnival itself.

Many modern carnivals are tacky, with rides of questionable safety, games in run-down aluminum trailers, and carnies who look like the cast of Deliverance, but this one seemed as if it had been magically transported from the past. Instead of trailers, there were painted wooden wagons that reminded me of old circus wagons. In the near distance was large wood structure with "Minotaur's Mirror Maze" and an illustration of a minotaur racing in fury down a corridor painted on the front. Closer at hand was a tilt-a-whirl, Madame Zoltan's tent, and another structure named, "The House of Wondrous Creatures," decorated with paintings of a bearded lady, an exceedingly tall man, a boy who resembled a werewolf, and Siamese twins.

When I looked beside me I noticed that Colin had his eyes closed and his hand extended.

"I feel something weird here, Marshall. It's almost as if I can sense ghosts and yet not. Do you see anything?"

"No. I haven't detected a single spirit here, which is peculiar. Ghosts often flock to carnivals, but not this one. I can feel something here too. It feels like a presence and yet... not."

I should probably explain that I possess the ability to see the dead, along with other psychic abilities. Colin could not see the dead as I could, but he could often feel their presence and his abilities were growing. Skye possessed the psychic abilities of a rock, but what he lacked in psychic ability, he made up for with courage and strength.

A child clown who could only be described as creepy walked past and grinned at us for a moment. I had never liked clowns, but the one at the entrance, and this boy, were especially disturbing. Something was very off about this carnival.

"It's kind of like a bad dream. Isn't it?" Colin said, gazing around.

"Yes, but people seem to be enjoying themselves."

It was true. Kids laughed and chased each other as they ran from ride to ride or ate cotton candy or corn dogs. Young couples walked in the Midway holding each other close, while older couples walked hand-in-hand. Boys Colin's age tried to impress girls by knocking down bowling pins with a baseball or shooting tin ducks. All around us, people were laughing and talking and having a wonderful time.

"It's a bit like stepping back in time, except for the people," Skye said.

"It reminds me of photos of carnivals in the 1930's."

Every structure, tent, and wagon looked like a relic from the past; faded and worn by the passing of time. I suppose that wasn't entirely unexpected. While there seemed to be far more vintage tents, signs, and other paraphernalia than I had ever seen before at a carnival or fair, it wasn't out of the question that a long-running carnival would retain much of its old equipment. Most might see it as a matter of economy or even nostalgia, but I suspected something far more sinister.

"What are we seeking?" Skye asked.

"If we knew, we would have already found it. People disappear when this carnival comes to town, and I high suspect it happens here. I don't think we need concern ourselves with victims being physically kidnapped. There is something supernatural at work here. We need to look for the peculiar."

"This whole carnival is peculiar."

"True, but while the tents and booths are from another era and the clowns are creepy, I don't believe they are the cause we're seeking. Something is capturing people, only not merely in the physical sense."

"The rides?"

"They are my main suspects. Somewhere in this carnival is something that truly does not belong."

"How do we narrow down the list? Ride the rides?" Colin asked.

"Yes, but together. There is safety in numbers. Together, I hope we'll be able to protect each other."

"So what do we try first?" Skye asked.

"My main suspect is the Minotaur's Mirror Maze. Let's begin there."

We walked across the Midway. The scent of cotton candy, hot buttered popcorn, and funnel cake made me hungry, but I wasn't sure it was wise to eat anything here. I was not that certain about my suspicions. Anything could be responsible for the disappearances. I might possibly be wrong about the carnival, but I did not believe so. Something had come to Verona that did not belong—something wicked.

Carnies generally had a bad reputation, perhaps because they came and went so quickly, and therefore were suspected of taking advantage of the naïve, then skipping out on the consequences. The reputation was no doubt largely undeserved, but the carnies of this particular carnival gave me the creeps, and that wasn't easy. There seemed to be an unusual number of clowns, and I was almost certain they were watching us. Everywhere we went, there was a clown gazing at us. And such clowns! They varied in age from quite young to very old. Each wore a worn costume that looked as if it belonged in another time. Most disturbing, each seemed more sinister than the last.

"Man, I hate clowns," Colin said.

"A lot of people do," Skye said.

"Really?"

"Yes, a significant number of people have clown-phobias."

"Do you?"

"Me? I fear nothing," Skye said with exaggerated bravado that made me smile. "Don't tell me *you're* afraid of clowns."

"I'm not afraid of them. I merely find them creepy. Part of me wants to punch them in the face."

That sounded typical of Colin and Skye.

We purchased tickets and walked inside a makeshift building. The interior was especially dark, almost too dark to see. I pulled out my phone to use my flashlight app. The screen went dark.

"Mine died too," Skye said. "Try your phone, Colin."

Colin pulled out his phone. The screen glowed but only for a few moments.

189

"I just charged this thing and I swear the bar went from fully charged to red as I watched it just now," Colin said.

"Something is sucking the batteries dry, but it's not spirits. I can't detect any."

"Maybe your psycho senses are on the blink," Skye said.

"That's psychic, not psycho," I said.

"Psychic to you. Psycho to me," Skye said, then laughed.

"Let's stick close together," I said.

The maze was confusing from the first moment. Every wall, the ceiling, and even the floor were mirrored. Many of the mirrors were similar to those found in a fun house; mirrors that made one appear skinny or fat, but as I gazed in these mirrors they made me look skeletal, ill, or corpse-like. I didn't like this maze at all.

We soon came to a branching corridor with three choices. I held out my hand and closed my eyes. Skye and Colin waited patiently. After a few moments, I confidently followed the passage to the right.

I used my mind, rather than my senses to guide me. The maze was designed to confound and confuse. What seemed the obvious route was often wrong, but also sometimes right so one could not use logic as a guide. I ignored logic and even intuition and instead relied on my psychic abilities.

"I just saw a clown," Colin said, punching his fist into his palm.

"I've seen them in the mirrors. These aren't normal mirrors," I said.

"Are they magic mirrors?" Skye asked.

"I wouldn't quite call them that, but they aren't far off."

"Mirror, mirror on the wall, who is the hottest guy of all," Skye asked, then grinned.

"Me! There is no question about that," Colin said.

"You two are absolutely hopeless. Most people would be scared right now."

"We're not most people," Skye said.

"That's surely the truth," I said.

As well as sensing the way forward, I searched for anything within the maze that was out of place or amiss. The overall atmosphere was sinister and watchful and yet I sensed no real danger here. What I felt was more the threat of harm and an almost sensual desire. The desire wasn't sexual and yet it was akin to it. I couldn't quite put my finger on it, but it was unwholesome. Nothing about Dr. Stupendous Smith's Carnival of Astonishment felt right.

We walked down passage after passage. The maze seemed too large to fit into the structure that housed it. That was perhaps an illusion, but perhaps not.

"This is very disorientating. It's hard to even keep my balance," Colin said.

"Don't look at the ceiling or the floor. It's easiest if you look straight ahead. Better yet, focus on me. I'm focusing on Marshall," Skye said.

"I knew you found me fascinating."

"Ha! Your only appeal is that you aren't a mirror."

"At the moment that makes me extremely appealing," I said.

"I'm not going to argue with that. It feels like we've been in here for hours, but we can't have been inside for more than fifteen minutes."

I kept moving forward at all times. There was no real danger here, but I didn't like the maze at all. I almost felt as if the Minotaur could appear at any moment to pursue us. The maze was not dangerous and yet I felt as if it could quickly become so.

I sensed we were nearing the exit and at the same moment I felt a force both curious and malevolent. Before me appeared the apparition of a man dressed all in black, wearing a black top hat, and carrying a black cane. He was not a spirit, nor a ghost. He was a living man and yet he was in front of me just long enough to tip his head toward me and then he vanished again. Perhaps his appearance was a trick of the mirrors, but I was almost sure that if I had reached out and touched him he would have been solid.

"Who was that?" Skye asked from behind me.

"I believe we just met Dr. Stupendous Smith."

I felt slightly nauseated as we continued on. I made the mistake of turning my head for a moment and came face-to-face with an image of my corpse laying in a casket. I quickly turned away. Death held no terror for me, but the image was still disturbing, more for the power that had made it appear than the image itself.

I breathed in the fresh air as we stepped outside.

"That was freaky," Colin said.

"What do you want to bet no one goes inside twice?" Skye asked.

"I wouldn't. It was fascinating but not what I'd call fun. I saw something especially weird in one of the mirrors," Colin said.

"What?" I asked.

"Me. Dead. What's more I looked blue and I was wet."

Skye and I looked at each other. Colin had nearly drowned when he was younger. Skye had saved him, but for a short time Colin had neither breath nor heartbeat. He had been dead.

"I saw myself in a casket," I said.

"I didn't see anything like that. After the first few moments I had the sense to look at only Marshall. I guess superior intelligence rules again."

"Superior intelligence, ha!" I said in my most sarcastic tone. "We can cross the Minotaur's Mirror Maze off our list. I don't believe there is any connection between it and the disappearances."

"What next then?"

"Let's try something that appears benign, the Ferris wheel."

The scents of corn dogs, freshly fried donuts, and kettle chips made me unusually hungry as we walked past several stands to get to the Ferris wheel. What was it about the food here? It seemed more than usually tempting, even for carnival food. I filed the fact away for further consideration. Perhaps it was a clue or perhaps I was merely hungry.

Across the lane, hucksters called out invitations to win prizes by throwing rings over bottles or plucking rubber ducks out of a flowing stream. The line for the Ferris wheel was not long, but I noticed a problem as we neared the front.

"We can't all fit in one," I said.

"Colin, you go with Marshall. I'll ride alone," Skye said.

"You sure?" I asked.

"If I can sit and wait calmly for The Mad Hatter to try to kill me, I think I can handle riding a Ferris wheel alone."

"Just don't complain to me if you disappear."

"How could I?" Skye asked.

"Be sure to take notes on where you end up if you do."

"You can suck the excitement out of anything, Marshall. I don't know who else could turn a disappearance into homework."

Colin and I climbed in a car. We arose a few feet into the air and then the wheel halted for Skye. We ascended and stopped, ascended and stopped until the wheel was filled with all new riders, then the ride truly began.

"This would be great for a date," Colin said as we rose up through the warm evening air.

"I suppose that would be more fun than riding with me," I said.

"You're fun in your own way."

"You can hold my hand if it will make you feel any better," I said with a grin.

"I'll think I'll pass."

"Oww, I'm wounded by rejection."

"What you are is a horrible actor."

"Yeah, that's all that's held me back from a theatre career—my total lack of acting talent."

"Man, you can see a long way from up here," Colin said as we reached the top.

"You can see the mansion," I said, pointing toward town. There in the distance, the upper two floors of Graymoor Mansion were visible above the trees.

"I'd like to see a big city from high up. Skye said New York looks incredible at night from a skyscraper."

"You'll get your chance I'm sure."

"It's on my list. I have a lot of plans."

"Hopefully, you'll have plenty of time to follow them all."

As we began to descend, I could see Skye in the next car. He had his arms spread out on the top of the seat. At least he hadn't disappeared so far.

Despite coming to the carnival to investigate, I enjoyed myself. This was my kind of carnival—spooky, mysterious, and bizarre. If it were not for the danger, I would have loved it.

The warm evening air rushed past we rode down, then up again. I could hear the music of the carousel coming from below and smell the mingled scents of buttered popcorn and funnel cake. The sound of laughter was in the air, along with an occasional scream, but they were not screams of terror, at least not terror inspired by real danger. There didn't seem to be any immediate threat here and yet each time this carnival visited Verona, people disappeared.

We rejoined Skye after our ride ended.

"Notice anything unusual?" Skye asked.

I shook my head.

"Marshall came onto me. He wanted to hold my hand. That's never happened before," Colin said.

Skye crossed his arms.

"Marshall, what did I tell you about putting the moves on my nephew?"

"Someone is twisting the facts a bit," I said, giving Colin a glare as he stood grinning. "Colin said the Ferris wheel would be a good ride for a date and I told him he could hold my hand if it would make him feel any better."

"I always suspected you were a predator," Skye said.

"Yeah, right. Now, if you two are done tormenting me we can move on."

"Are we done?" Skye asked Colin.

"I suppose."

"You guys need to stick to working out. You're not that funny."

Skye moved his hand in a so-so gesture. Colin laughed.

I gazed around trying to decide what to check out next. It's especially hard to find something when one does not know what he is seeking. What could make people disappear? How is it accomplished? Where does it happen?

We walked by the pavilion of Marco the Magnificent, where a young man stood outside and swallowed fire as a small crowd watched. I gazed at the large sign on the side of the building behind him, which read, "Marco the Magnificent—Swallower of Fire and Sword."

That made me think of a magician, but Marco was no magician. I gazed about to see if could spot one among the pavilions, tents, and small structures and stages, but there was none; so much for that idea. It was a bit obvious too.

"I'm starving. Can we get something to eat?" Colin asked.

"I'm not sure how safe it is," I said.

"There doesn't seem to any danger," Skye said, indicating everyone eating around us. "What do you expect? Poison?"

"I suspect everything about this carnival. Perhaps I'm being paranoid. I think just one of us should try something so the others can watch over him."

"I will be the guinea pig. I have to have some cotton candy," Colin said.

"It's your call," I said, looking at Skye.

"Maybe I should try it first," he said.

"Come on, Skye. I've faced greater danger than being poisoned by cotton candy."

"Okay. You win."

We walked together toward the food booths. The fact that everything from the corn dogs to the fried donuts smelled especially good made me uneasy.

Colin stepped away from the vendor with a huge puff of blue cotton candy on a paper stick.

"No pink?" I asked.

"The blue tastes better. Blue M&Ms taste better too. I don't care what *anyone* says," Colin said, looking at Skye pointedly.

"I'm sorry, the red M&Ms are clearly the best," Skye said.

"Not even close!"

"So this is the kind of intellectual discussion you two get into?" I asked.

"Last night we were arguing about quantum physics," Skye said.

"Skye thinks quantum entanglement isn't possible. Can you believe that?" Colin asked.

I eyed them both. I was fairly sure they were putting me on, but I wasn't entirely sure.

"Come on, let's get away from the food. The scents are driving me crazy," I said.

"You'd love the cotton candy. It's sooo good," Colin said, taking a big bite.

"Grrr."

We walked around the carnival, observing games and rides, watching for anything amiss. We rode the scrambler and this time I was the odd man out. I was glad I hadn't eaten anything for I feared it might have reappeared as I was jerked this way and that.

We hit the tilt-a-whirl next. I loved that ride as a kid. We were all able to fit into one car together, but I made the mistake of getting in the middle. As the ride started and the car began to spin, Skye and Colin alternated leaning hard into me. I was smaller than them both so I was quite squashed. The pair enjoyed squishing me between them. They could be quite evil at times.

It might have been my imagination, but everywhere we went clowns watched us. I had noted it all along, but now there seemed to be more of them. Did they know why we were here? Their gazes were not friendly. Only when they interacted with children did they seem pleasant, and even then there was something fake and creepy about their demeanor. I felt as if I was watching a predator offering a child candy to get into his car. I shuddered. Everyone at the carnival was prey.

My sense of danger grew as we approached the carousel. It was a beautiful work of art with hand-carved and hand-painted horses, circus animals, and chariots. The calliope music was enchantingly beautiful.

As I had with the other rides, I observed this one closely. I watched the riders choose their mounts and then climb on. Many of the riders were kids, but there were plenty of older people too, even a couple who were likely in their eighties. Everyone loved the carousel.

The carousel began to move and soon it kept pace with the music. The hundreds and hundreds of lights made it all the more enchanting.

I picked out three targets and watched them—the old couple, a teen boy in a red shirt, and a young girl who rode a unicorn as her father stood beside her. I could not begin to observe everyone, so I kept my eye on my targets each time they came into view.

The carousel went around and around. The old couple smiled and held hands as they sat together in a stationary chariot. The teen boy eyed girls who were riding nearby. The young girl laughed with delight.

"Oh! So many colors!" Colin said.

I turned to look at him for a moment, but only a moment. Colin grinned goofily and held his hands out as if trying to touch the light of the carousel. Skye was watching him closely, so I concentrated on the task at hand.

My targets were enjoying themselves and why not? I examined them as closely as possible, going so far as to brush their surface thoughts with my mind. I had the ability to read emotions as well as some thoughts. I wasn't exactly what I'd call a mind reader, and yet I had abilities along those lines. I didn't make a habit of getting into people's heads because I considered it unethical, but sometimes my talent helped my investigations. I always knew when someone was lying. Perhaps that's why no one would play poker with me. Regardless, my ability allowed me to more closely monitor my targets than I could otherwise. I only saw each for a few seconds before they disappeared from view again, but I could maintain contact with their minds.

For the moment, I focused on the boy. He was about fifteen and he was entranced by the colors of the carousel, just like Colin. He continued to gaze at the girls, but he looked all around him with a sense of wonder. I closed my eyes for a moment and focused, trying to see what he did. Soon, I could see the interior of the carousel and lights that left long distorted trails of color. Everything went in and out of focus. The boy had either been drinking, was high or... I turned to look at Colin again. I brushed his mind with my own. I sensed the same chaotic thoughts and I knew Colin had not been drinking and did not do drugs.

I turned to focus on the boy again. I waited for him to appear, but his horse was empty as it came into view again. I watched closely as the carousel turned and brought his horse around once more, but the boy had gone missing. I searched for him with my mind, but he was gone.

I looked back toward Colin. He swayed slightly. Skye stepped in beside him.

"I think we'd better leave," I said for I sensed Colin was in danger.

"Hey. Hey. Let's get some more cotton candy. You gotta try it," Colin said, gazing at Skye and then me. If I didn't know better I'd think he was drunk.

"I think you've had enough. It's time to go home," Skye said.

"Aww, Skye! Come on!"

"Maybe we'll come back tomorrow."

"Yes!"

Skye and I walked on each side of Colin to keep him from swaying and also to make sure he didn't topple over. The clowns eyed us as we crossed the Midway. I could feel them watching us as we departed. I sensed their displeasure that we had escaped or more precisely that Colin had escaped. I was right to be paranoid about the food. I knew that now.

I feared Colin would grow more incoherent, but instead he grew more lucid. Skye took him up to their suite when we arrived back at the mansion. I went into the kitchen and asked Martha for a pot of London Cuppa tea and some cookies. When it was prepared, I carried it up to the fourth floor, where the entrance to the suite of rooms shared by Skye and Colin were located.

An enormous painting concealed the entrance. Anyone who didn't know the doorway was there would not have guessed. Behind the painting was a short flight of ancient stairs that led into the main room of the suite.

"I'm here and I'm exhausted," I called out.

"You really need to hit the gym if carrying a bit of tea wears you out," Skye said.

"Hey, it's like half a mile up here and most of it is stairs."

"You'd have made a wonderful photographer the way you enlarge everything."

"Have we been watching *Good Neighbors* again?" I asked.

"Damn, I thought I could pass that off as my creation."

"Not likely, Skye. You know you shouldn't try to be clever."

"I'll forgive you for that since you have cookies."

"How's Colin?"

"I'm better. I'm not seeing things anymore," Colin said as he entered from his bedroom.

"Come and have some tea. It will help."

"Marshall has never been the same since he spent those years in England. He thinks tea cures everything."

"It does for the most part."

"See?"

We sat down before the fireplace, drank tea, and ate cookies. I loved this room. The armchairs and loveseat in front of the fire were Victorian, but the rest of the room looked like something out of the Renaissance. In fact, it was. The entire room had been moved from Europe when the mansion was built. The Graymoor's must have been loaded.

"You mentioned colors. What did you see?" I asked after Colin had drunk some of the strong tea.

"I could see streams of light coming from each of the lights on the carousel and I could see individual colors, like a rainbow. The streams flowed and moved."

"I was watching a boy riding the carousel. I tapped into his mind to see what he was seeing. You're describing the same thing."

"I felt strange and it looked like the horses and other animals on the carousel were moving. I don't mean moving up and down, but moving their legs and turning their heads."

"It sounds like the cotton candy was a hallucinogen," Skye said.

"Something in it certainly was. I'm beginning to put together a picture of how the disappearances occur. The food at the carnival, at least some of it, is laced with a hallucinogen. When someone under its influence rides the carousel, he or she disappears. Perhaps other rides are involved too, but the carousel is at the bottom of this."

"How do you know?" Skye asked.

"Because the boy I was watching disappeared. He was there and then the next time his horse came around he was gone."

"He could have simply left the ride."

"No, it was going too fast. Even if he wanted to try it, he couldn't have managed it that quickly. He was taken, like the others."

"How?"

"That I don't know. I'd like to get a look at that carousel."

"Let's go back after the carnival closes and check it out," Colin said.

"Skye and I will go back. You will stay here."

"Oh, come on."

"I won't risk it, especially since you've come under the influence of cotton candy."

"It's wearing off. I'm mostly fine now."

"No. We are not taking the chance," Skye said.

Colin looked at Skye as if he was about to protest, but then closed his mouth. He knew better than to argue.

***

I opened my door when Skye knocked on it lightly at 2 a.m.

"You ready?" Skye asked.

"Always."

We were both dressed in black to blend into the darkness, but I must admit Skye looked much better than I did. He was wearing a skin-tight outfit that made him look like a Ninja. I merely looked like a guy dressed in black.

"I see you brought your sword. You'll use any excuse to carry that thing, won't you?"

"You've been glad I've had this sword with me on plenty of occasions," Skye said.

"True enough."

We made our way quietly through the mansion. At this hour, it was unlikely anyone would be up and about.

"It's a nasty night for this," Skye said as we exited through the kitchen door.

"All the better to conceal us."

It was a nasty night—period. The wind whipped rain into our faces as we ran to the old carriage house. Thunder rumbled and lightning flashed. We climbed in my hearse and drove toward the edge of town.

We parked well away from the carnival. The rain fell steadily as we made our way onto the grounds. All was dark and silent except for the nearly continuous thunder and flashes of bright lightning directly overhead.

I followed Skye as he led the way silently through the Midway. The tent flaps were closed, all the lights were out, and there was no sign of even a single clown, but if anything, the carnival was even eerier than it had been when we visited hours before.

Canvas was drawn around the carousel to protect it from the elements and it needed protection on this night. The rain poured down and Skye and I were both completely soaked.

I was relieved to be out of the rain when we slipped between the canvas flaps. Only then did we turn on our flashlights.

"You think anyone saw us?" Skye asked.

"No. I didn't detect anyone in the vicinity," I said, tapping the side of my head. Possessing psychic abilities had its advantages.

The carousel animals appeared sinister in the dim light and almost seemed to come to life when the lightning flashed outside. I remembered Colin's hallucinations and gazed at the horses, dragons, and other creatures uneasily.

We made our way quickly to the center and found a small door that gave us access to the mechanical workings of the carousel. We closed ourselves inside.

"Do you know what you're looking for?" Skye asked as he shined his light on the mass of pistons and gears.

"Something that doesn't belong."

"Do you know what doesn't belong? This isn't exactly a car engine."

I silently walked around the machine. I spotted nothing out of place until there was a deafening clap of thunder overhead and the small space was brilliantly illuminated by a bolt of lightning that followed a rod down into the machine and caused a large vertical cylinder to shine with brilliant light.

"That doesn't belong," I said when I had recovered from the shock.

"You think?"

Skye and I now focused on the mechanism at the top of the gears and pistons that operated the carousel.

"It's obvious that the cylinder stores energy, like a giant super-powerful battery. The energy travels along those conduits," I said, following them with my flashlight. "I have to get a closer look."

I began to climb a ladder that led to a catwalk that surrounded the upper part of the machine.

"Are you sure that's wise. That thing is made to attract lightning."

"Oh, it's not wise at all, but it is necessary. You can stay down there if you're scared."

"Yeah, right," Skye said, climbing on the ladder and following me.

We stepped onto the catwalk. I didn't care for heights, but Skye seemed perfectly at ease. I traced the conduits with my flashlight. Whatever this thing was; it was complicated.

"You have any idea how it works?" Skye asked.

"Dammit, Jim. I'm a psychic investigator, not a mechanic."

Skye laughed. I knew he'd get the Dr. McCoy reference. "This thing looks like it belongs on the Enterprise," Skye said.

"Yes, except that it uses nineteenth and early twentieth century parts. This is damn peculiar. The conduits channel power to this bit that looks like a toaster with tentacles. The conduits leading out of it go out into the carousel and I bet each one hooks into one of the poles the animals slide up and down on."

"The big question is; what does it do?" Skye said.

I walked around further and spotted another large canister. It too glowed with light, or rather scores of lights. I closed my eyes and extended my hand toward it. I concentrated, but couldn't detect what was inside.

"Hold onto me," I said.

Skye grabbed my belt as I leaned out over the catwalk. I closed my eyes again and concentrated as I reached out. My fingers tingled as they touched the surface. It wasn't a physical surface at all. It was pure energy. I pushed against it and concentrated harder. My eyes popped open and I would have fallen if Skye wasn't holding me. He pulled me back onto the catwalk.

"What's wrong?"

"I know where all those who have gone missing are—they're in there," I said, pointing to the cylinder.

"You mean their spirits are trapped inside?"

"Not just their spirits, their bodies too."

"How is that possible? That cylinder is barely big enough to hold one body."

I gave Skye my *Really? You have to ask?* look.

"Oh. Right. So how do we get them out? Destroy the machine?"

"That would be risky. They are still alive in there. If they were merely spirits it would be different, but it may be possible to restore them."

"How?"

"That cylinder isn't physical. It's composed of energy."

"Like a force field?"

"Yes. We need to cut off its power supply. If we do..."

"You'll kill them all."

Skye and I quickly turned. A man dressed entirely in black climbed the ladder and stepped onto the catwalk.

"Dr. Stupendous Smith, I presume?" I said.

He nodded his head. "I'm afraid I can't allow you to shut down the force field I believe you called it? Yes, I like that. That's a good name for it. You see, we have need of the energy of those spirits."

I focused my mind upon the doctor. He was a living being, but he was also..."

"You're dead," I said.

Skye looked back at me for just a moment with disbelief on his features.

"Technically correct, yes, but thanks to this device I'm as good as alive, don't you think?"

"What you've done is monstrous," I said.

The doctor shrugged. "Perhaps. I'm afraid I will have to ask the two of you to stay and join the others."

"Not likely," Skye said.

I could hear rustling below. I looked down and spotted the clowns climbing the ladders to the catwalk.

"Stay close," Skye said. I was suddenly very glad he had his sword.

"I do hope you aren't going to make things difficult. I'm afraid you won't be able to kill us. One cannot kill what is already dead."

I peered into the doctor's mind. I had no reservations about doing so. He gave no outward sign of it, but he was afraid. I nodded subtly at Skye when he glanced at me. Skye smiled. He lived for moments like this.

The clowns were on the catwalk now. They were like the doctor, alive and yet dead. Skye and I moved so that we were back-to-back. The clowns grinned, sensing weakness, but they were sorely mistaken.

I turned my head toward Skye and whispered, "The next time the lightning strikes, destroy the machine."

"I'm so glad you've come to join us. You'll make a valuable addition to our collection. Each new addition adds to our strength."

"How long have you been collecting?" I asked. I wanted to get as much information from the doctor as possible and already the thunder was rumbling loudly overhead. We were nearly out of time.

"Since the 1830's. It was difficult in the beginning. It took time to perfect my wonderful machine. Impressive, don't you think?"

Lightning struck. The chamber we stood in was filled with light so blinding I could not see, but I could feel Skye snap into action. He thrust his sword into the heart of the machine. The force of the resulting explosion thrust me off the platform, but even as I fell Skye wrapped his arms around me. We smashed against the wall, with Skye taking the bulk of the impact. We slid to the floor and looked up at the tangled mass.

The chamber was dark for only a moment. Hundreds of small points of light exploded outward, then all was dark once again. We were alone. Dr. Stupendous Smith and his clowns, which moments before had been both alive and dead, were now only dead.

Skye and I exited the chamber, walked across the platform of the carousel and out into the storm. Skye's sword had returned to him. It was one of its powers. Another was that it was unbreakable. Any other sword would not have survived being thrust into the gears of the machine, but Skye's sword could do so with ease.

We didn't speak as we hurried back to the hearse. When we slipped into the car Skye and I took one look at each other and laughed. Despite being wet, Skye's hair was standing out at odd angles and his face was smeared with black.

"You look ridiculous," he said.

"Take a look in the mirror."

Skye pulled down the mirror and peered at himself.

"Yikes! I am still gorgeous, but yikes!"

I rolled my eyes, started the car, and headed back to Graymoor Mansion.

***

I slept in the next morning. After breakfast, I drove back to the carnival. The carousel, tents, and structures were still there. The sheriff's car was parked at the edge of the field as well as three state police cars. The sheriff stepped toward me as I drew close to the police tape that blocked off the site.

"Why am I not surprised to see you, Marshall? Do you have a psychic sense that attracts you to crime scenes?"

"This isn't a crime scene."

"You haven't seen the inside of the carousel. There are skeletons everywhere and the works are a mess."

"I know."

"You know?"

"Skye and I were here last night. Well, super early this morning actually."

"Why doesn't that surprise me either?"

I grinned. "Let me get you up to speed," I said and began to tell the sheriff what had transpired in the early morning hours.

"Damn, how am I going to write this one up?" he asked when I'd finished.

"You'll think of something."

"I would almost rather it had remained an unsolved mystery."

"Leave it at that then. Believe me, no one is going to be able to figure out what happened here."

"No kidding. We've got skeletons, but only skeletons. It looks more like an archaeological site in there than a crime scene. Some of the state boys think it's an elaborate prank. We're checking with universities to see if any of them are missing skeletons from their medical department."

"Go with that then. Write it down as a prank. See? There are lots of ways to write your report. I could have left you in the dark, but I thought you'd want to know the truth."

"I appreciate it, although sometimes ignorance is bliss. So you say at least one boy disappeared off the carousel last night?"

"Yes. Did you get any missing persons reports?"

"No, but it has only been a few hours."

"The boy I saw disappear was about fifteen. I would think his parents would be rather frantic by now. It's curious they haven't reported him missing, but I have a theory about that."

"Care to share it?"

"Let me check something out and I'll get back to you."

"Okay, but if this turns into a missing person case it's going to get a lot more complicated."

I returned to my hearse and drove straight back to Graymoor. I climbed the stairs to my room and pulled out the file the director of the Verona Historical Society Museum had sent over as well as my notes.

I checked my notes and turned to the 1958 issue of *The Verona Citizen* in the file. There was no mention of disappearances. Eight people, six of them children, had disappeared in three days during May of that year. I had written the names and ages in my notes, but the information was completely missing from the paper. I turned to the 1933 issue next and found the same thing. History, or at least a small part of it, had changed. I checked the issues for 1883, 1908, and 1983. There was no mention of even a single disappearance in any of the newspapers. My suspicion was correct. I called the sheriff and gave him the good news.

***

I spent the day after our encounter with Dr. Stupendous Smith tying up loose ends. Much of the day was spent in research. I searched for the names of a few of the formerly missing persons in later editions of *The Verona Citizen* and found enough to prove my theory beyond a reasonable doubt. The lack of missing person reports in newspapers that previously contained the reports proved my suspicion correct, but I wanted to be as certain of the facts as possible. I was satisfied and considered the case closed.

One of the advantages of living in The Graymoor Mansion B&B was the food. Breakfast, lunch, and supper were served in the main dining room daily. Bed & breakfast really wasn't the correct name for the hotel. It was truly a bed, breakfast, lunch, and supper, but that would have made for a rather awkward name.

I was certain Skye would want to know what I discovered and knew Colin and Sean would be interested as well so I invited them to join me in a private dining room for supper.

I arrived to find Sean already seated. Covered dishes with place cards were already on the table, as well as filled glasses and pitchers of iced-tea and water. I took my place.

"I take it there was some excitement last night?" Sean asked.

"Merely a few undead clowns, trapped souls, and some rather wicked lightning. You know, the usual sort of thing."

Sean raised an eyebrow.

"Skye and I will fill you in when we're all here, but first I want to eat. I'm starving."

I lifted the lid off my plate to reveal my choices from this evening's buffet. I had selected meat loaf, baked beans, and sour cream au Gratian potatoes.

"Fine, don't wait for us," Skye said as he entered with Colin.

"You're late," I said.

"Barely."

"Well I'm hungry."

Skye and Colin sat at their places and everyone took off the covers.

"A salad?" I asked, looking at Skye's plate.

"I love Caesar salad and it has chicken on it. You don't think this level of gorgeousness is effortless, do you?"

"Oh lord."

"You should spend less time playing with Casper the Unfriendly Ghost and more time in the gym. You could become at least a little gorgeous, Marshall," Skye said.

"Hey, we both played with Casper last night."

"Perverts," Colin said, then laughed.

"What went on last night? You mentioned the undead. Are you talking zombies?" Sean asked. "What was it this time? Is there a voodoo witch doctor wreaking havoc? A Druid curse?"

"None of the above," I said, trying to eat.

"I'd like to know what happened too since I wasn't allowed to go. Did you see the creepy clowns again?" Colin asked.

"I wanted to wait until we had eaten to tell you, but obviously you can't wait," I said.

Skye and I filled Sean and Colin in on the details of the night before. Both listened closely, but did not act surprised. They were both well accustomed to supernatural events.

"Ah man! I could so have come with you! That is the last time you are leaving me out of the fun! You ruined the carnival too. I wanted to go back," Colin said.

"The carnival is still there, but there is no one to run it."

"What do you think will happen to it?" Sean asked.

I shrugged. "There certainly aren't any heirs. Perhaps the town will keep it."

"Where do you think all the trapped spirits went?" Colin asked.

"Ah. That's the best part. I've saved it until last. I grew suspicious when the sheriff told me no one had been reported missing so I spent most of the day in my room doing research."

Colin made a show of yawning. I smacked him in the back of the head, but he only laughed.

"The research might not be exciting, but what I discovered is this; the disappearances that had been noted in past editions of the newspapers were missing. I researched a little further and found some of the formerly missing persons mentioned in later editions of *The Verona Citizen*. When we released those who were trapped, I believe they were returned to the moment in time they were taken. For them, it's as if nothing happened to them at all."

"What about Dr. Stupendous Smith and the creepy-ass clowns?" Colin asked.

"I believe they are gone for good. When we released the trapped souls, the doctor and all the others disintegrated into piles of bones. I'm still not sure exactly how that device worked, but thanks to Skye it will never work again."

"I'm always happy to lend a hand when it comes to destruction."

"You just like to use your sword."

"Hey, how often do I get to use a sword in this world? Damn I miss Tydannon. Remember when we were about to be massacred on the bridge above..."

I grinned. Skye was quite the swashbuckler. I was finally able to eat while Skye retold his favorite tale. I had no doubt that someday he would return to Tydannon, but until then I was certain we would have plenty of adventures together.

71118945R00125

Made in the USA
Middletown, DE
29 September 2019